THE GUNSMITH

484

To Steal from the Dead

THE GUNSMITH

484

To Steal from the Dead

J.R. Roberts

SPEAKING VOLUMES, LLC
NAPLES, FLORIDA
2023

To Steal from the Dead

ISBN 978-1-64540-999-1

Chapter One

Kansas City

Clint Adams had been in Kansas many times over the years. This time he was passing through, returning from an expedition to the South, to track down a killer. He meant to bring the man back to Kansas to hang, but it was a man's choice to slap leather with the Gunsmith, resulting in the outlaw's death.

Clint had reported the success of his hunt by telegraph but had no desire to physically return to the town where the man's crime had been committed. The man killed had been a friend of Clint's, and he preferred to move on, so he bypassed the town of Jensen and stopped in Kansas City.

Kansas City grew by leaps and bounds each time Clint returned there. It was no longer referred to as the "town" of Kansas City. Now it was a "city" with all the trappings that went with that reference. It had a modern police department, paved streets and positions for many politicians to fight over.

Clint had no interest in politics. But he had been away from serious poker games for some time and intended to reacquaint himself with the game.

Kansas City probably had more than 25 saloons, 8 gambling houses, and was quite proud of their new Boot Hill. The first town to institute a Boot Hill was Hays, Kansas. But it didn't take long for the usage of the name to spread to other towns.

As he usually did upon arrival, he boarded his horse at a large livery, then went looking for a hotel. Several ones had been erected since Clint's last visit to Kansas City. He chose The Raphael Hotel and got himself a second floor room that did not overlook the plaza where it was located.

With that done, he went looking for a good meal, which would be followed by a visit to some of the gambling houses and saloons. Recent time spent in the company of his friend, Bat Masterson, had reawakened his interest in poker. Bat, and their friend, Luke Short, had always told Clint he should play the game professionally. They considered that he had all the natural instincts. He figured spending time at the tables would require less use of his gun.

He found a likely looking café and turned his attention to a steak supper.

***

"Sheriff, you have to help me!" the woman pleaded.

Sheriff Zack Wilson sat back in his chair and regarded the lady who had burst into his office. He listened to her complaint and then shook his head.

"There's nothin' I can do, Mrs. Lake," he told her. "Hays is out of my jurisdiction. Why don't you go to the new police station and tell them your problem?"

"I did," she said, "and they told me the same thing."

"Then go back to the Hays sheriff," Wilson suggested.

"I spent three days badgering him," she said. "He insists I prove my charge."

"Then do that," Wilson said.

"I can't," Sally Lake said. "I can't prove anything!"

"Then it seems to me you're out of luck, Ma'am," the sheriff said, and stood. "Now if you'll excuse me, I have rounds to make."

Sally Lake had lived in Kansas City long enough to know that the sheriff's "rounds" always involved a stop at a poker table.

"I'll walk you out," he said.

He escorted her out the front door, then turned and locked it.

"Once again, I'm sorry I can't help you," he said, and walked away.

Sally wanted to run after him, screaming, but restrained herself. She would wait for him to get comfortable at a table, and then hound him again. But to do that she would have to find the game he had chosen.

***

Sheriff Wilson walked to The Red Spade Gambling house. It was early enough in the day for him to find an empty chair at one of the poker tables.

"Gentlemen," he greeted, as he seated himself.

"Sheriff, glad to see you," Bill Cadman said. "We were afraid you weren't gonna make it."

"You never have to worry about that, Bill," Wilson said. "The Town Council made it real clear they don't expect much from me, anymore. Not with that new police station."

"I guess you're glad they're still payin' you," Cadman said.

"Well, since you're on the council, Bill, I know you had a lot to do with that, so you could take the money back at the tables."

"Come on, Sheriff," Jeff McCallum said. "You could always win."

"I think we all know better than that," Wilson said.

The fourth man at the table was unknown to Wilson.

"If you know you're going to lose, Sheriff, why do you play?" that man asked.

"I like playin'," Sheriff Wilson said. "Whether I win or not."

"Sheriff," Bill Cadman said, "meet Clint Adams."

The sheriff stared at Clint with wide, shocked eyes.

Chapter Two

Earlier, Clint had finished his steak and went out in search of a friendly poker table. He found his way to The Red Spade Gambling House. It had a large, red Queen of Spades above the door. When he entered, he found the same true on the walls around him. He was sure the owner had a good reason to turn the black spade to red. Maybe he would find out what it was, eventually, but at the moment he was interested in a poker table that had four players seated at it. He bought some chips from a cashier just inside the door.

As he approached the table, he saw one man stand and say, "Deal me out."

They passed each other, one heading for the bar and one for the table.

"You fellas mind if I sit in?" he asked.

"If you don't mind the stakes bein' kind of high, have a seat."

From the look of the chips on the table, Clint knew his idea of high stakes was quite different from theirs.

"I think I can handle it," Clint said, seating himself and setting his chips on the table.

"I'm Bill Cadman," one man said, "that's Jeff McCallum." Both men wore suits and Clint figured them for local businessmen. The suits were not the kind any self-respecting professional gambler would wear. For one thing, Bat Masterson would never be caught dead in a grey suit.

"We don't know this fella's name," Cadman said, indicating the third man with a nod of his head.

"A name ain't important," the third man said. "Just the game."

"That's true enough," Clint said, as the nameless man dealt, "but just to keep it friendly, I'm Clint Adams."

The man dealing paused.

"What the hell is the Gunsmith doin' playin' poker in Kansas City?"

"Does it matter where I play?" Clint asked. "After all, the only important thing is the game."

The third man, dressed in trail clothes, finished dealing and said, "I guess you have a point."

"I hope you're not here lookin' for trouble," Cadman said. "I manage the bank, and Jeff, here, is a lawyer. We're not lookin' to be around when lead starts to fly."

"That's fine with me," Clint said. "I'm just looking to let the chips fly."

"The bet's yours, Adams," the nameless man said.

"I'll open for fifty," Clint said.

"That's a pretty moderate bet, Mr. Adams," Cadman observed.

Clint smiled and said, "I'm just getting started."

***

Clint had noticed the badge on Zack Wilson's chest as the sheriff entered. The nameless man noticed it, too, and quickly said, "Deal me out," then headed for the bar. Clint noticed he wore a gun and holster like a man who knew how to use them. He obviously had no desire to play at a table with a lawman.

Wilson picked up the cards and began to shuffle.

"Sheriff, aren't you interested in what brings the Gunsmith to Kansas City?" Cadman said.

"Not at all," Wilson said. "Let your new police department worry about that. Whatever he's doin' here ain't gonna concern me."

He dealt out the cards and they concentrated on their hands. Clint was very happy not to have to verbally fence with the lawman.

***

Later a serving girl came to the table to take drink orders. The two Town Council members ordered whiskey, while the sheriff settled for a beer,

"Anythin' for you, sir?" the girl asked Clint.

"No thanks," he said. "I don't drink while I'm playing poker."

As the girl withdrew, Cadman said to Wilson, "There you go, Sheriff. Take a page out of the Gunsmith's book. Don't drink when you play. Maybe you'll have better luck."

"As a matter of fact," Clint said, "not drinking doesn't change your luck, it just keeps your eyes sharp to see what's going on around the table. And it sure as hell doesn't change the cards that come to you, just how you play them."

"It don't matter," Wilson said. "I don't get drunk and play the cards I get. I just play 'em wrong, sober or not."

"I still don't understand how you can play with that attitude," Clint said.

"The sheriff just likes to contribute," McCallum said.

"Yes," Cadman said, "we just take his money and put it right back into the city."

"You still call your council the 'town' council," Clint asked, "even though Kansas City is more city than town?"

"We're gonna have a Town Council meetin' about that," McCallum said.

At that point a woman came through the batwing doors and stormed over to the table.

"Sheriff, I just can't take no for an answer," she blurted.

Clint noticed that even angry the thirtyish woman was quite lovely.

"Mrs. Lake," Wilson said, "I'm not in my office, at the moment. But even if I was, there's still nothin' I can do for you."

"But you're the law!"

"In Kansas City, yes, but not in Hays."

"That's ridiculous, the law's the law."

"It doesn't work that way, Ma'am," Wilson said. "Now please, I'm tryin' to concentrate."

The woman looked like she was about to cry, whirled around and stormed out of the place.

"What's her problem?" Cadman asked.

"She had some trouble in Hays, and she wants me to solve it."

"And there's nothing at all you can do for her?" Clint asked.

"The sheriff barely has any authority here," McCallum said. "What's he gonna do in Hays?"

"Forget about it," Wilson said, "Somebody deal."

Chapter Three

Clint could certainly see not only how bad Zack Wilson's luck was, but what a bad player he was, as well. For that matter the two Town Council members did not play much better.

"That's it for me," Sheriff Wilson finally said. "I got rounds to make."

"I'll cash out also," Clint said. How about I buy you a drink, Sheriff, before you start your rounds?"

"Suits me," Wilson said, and they both went to the bar. When they each had a beer, Clint asked the question that had been on his mind all night.

"Tell me about this lady's trouble in Hays, Sheriff."

"Oh, that?" Wilson said. "She says her husband died while they were in Hays, coming back from a vacation in St. Louis."

"Did somebody kill him?"

"No, no nothin' like that," the lawman said. "It was pretty clear he died of a heart attack. He was about twenty years older than his wife."

"So what's the problem?"

"She's sure the undertaker stole her husband's wallet and jewelry," Wilson explained. "Only she can't prove it."

"She went to the sheriff there?"

"She did, but he said there was no evidence."

"So, she came here for help and got none," Clint said.

Wilson finished his beer and set the empty mug down.

"Like I told her, out of my jurisdiction."

"Right."

"Thanks for the drink," Wilson said, "and the poker lesson."

"You're welcome."

The sheriff turned to leave, but Clint had one more question.

"Before you go," he said, "where can I find this Mrs. Lake?"

"What's your interest?"

"I don't have a problem with proper jurisdiction."

"That's true," Wilson said. "Her husband owned the General Store. You'll find her there."

"Okay, thanks."

Wilson left, and Clint finished his beer before heading for his hotel and a good night's sleep.

***

In the morning, after a decent breakfast in the hotel dining room, he went looking for the General Store. He found it on Main Street, in and among a line of others, such as a leather works, a hardware store, an apothecary, and a lady's hat shop.

He entered the store, which had apparently just opened. There were no customers, but there was a young man behind the counter.

"You're in luck, friend," he said. "We just opened. What can I do for you?"

"I'd like to see Mrs. Lake."

"Mrs. Lake just lost her husband," the young man said. "She's in mournin' and can't see anyone."

"I'm here about her husband's death," Clint said. "Tell her my name's Clint Adams."

"Adams . . . the Gunsmith?" the young man asked, going pale.

"That's right."

"Um, wait right here," the young clerk said, and hurried toward the back. In a few minutes he returned.

"Um, Mrs. Lake lives upstairs," he said. "There's a staircase in the rear of the store. She said for you to go right up."

"Thanks."

Clint walked to the back of the store, located the stairway and walked up. When he got to the door, he knocked. Sally Lake opened it dressed in a simple blue dress that did not exactly look like widow's weeds. Her long, dark hair was perfectly in place, hanging almost to her shoulders.

"Mr. Adams. Please, come in."

"Thank you."

He entered, and she closed and locked the door.

"Can I offer you something?" she asked. "Coffee or tea?"

"Coffee would be nice."

"Please, make yourself comfortable. I'll be right back."

"Thanks."

The neat sitting room was furnished with a plush sofa, a matching armchair and a coffee table. He saw very little indication that a married couple lived there.

She came from the kitchen carrying a tray with a coffee pot and cups. She set the tray down on the table, then sat next to him on the sofa and poured two cups.

"Thank you," he said, when she handed him one.

"Now, what brings you here?" she asked.

"I couldn't help hearing the conversation you had last night with the sheriff."

"You mean the confrontation?"

15

"Yes."

"I'm sorry you saw that. I'm not usually so . . . strident, but no one is making any effort to help me."

"That's why I'm here to see you," Clint told her. "Suppose you tell me what this problem is that no one will help you with?"

"Why would you care?" she asked.

"I often ask myself the same question," Clint said, "but it seems when I find someone in need of help, I can't help but get curious."

"Well," she said, "all right. My husband and I went to St. Louis to celebrate our twentieth wedding anniversary. I was very young when we married, and he was considerably older than I. On the way back we got to Hays, signed into a hotel to get a good night's sleep before continuing. When I woke the next morning, he was lying next to me . . . dead."

"I'm so sorry."

"The local doctor said he died of a heart attack. I was distraught and didn't know what to do. The doctor had the body removed to the undertaker, and before I knew it, he'd been buried."

"You didn't know?"

"The doctor gave me a sedative," she said "When I awoke it was all over. He was gone."

"I can understand why that would be hard to deal with," Clint said.

Chapter Four

"What did you do then?"

"I went to the undertaker to get my husband's personal belongings."

"And?"

"They were gone."

"All of them?"

"Most of them. My husband always carried a lot of money, and he liked flashy things—a watch, a diamond stickpin. Those items were gone, and his wallet was empty."

"What did the undertaker say happened to it all?"

"He claimed he gave me everything," she said. "The wallet was empty except for some photos and ticket stubs."

"What happened then?"

"I accused the undertaker of stealing everything."

"How did he react?"

"He very calmly told me if I believed that, I should go to the sheriff. So I did."

"And what did he do?"

"He told me I needed evidence to prove that the undertaker stole everything. Without it there was nothing he could do."

"He didn't even question the man?"

"No," she said. "In fact, he seemed afraid of him."

"Afraid of an undertaker?"

"He seems to be a very respected man in Hays."

"But he steals from the dead."

"Why would my husband be the only one?" she asked. "He seemed so calm when I accused him, that I'm sure he's done it before."

"What did you do next?"

"What could I do? I came back here and talked to Sheriff Wilson."

"And?"

"He said there was nothing he could do because Hays was out of his jurisdiction. Then he went to play poker."

"An undertaker who steals from the dead seems to be a very serious problem."

"That's what I thought," she said, "but I'm not getting any help. I thought about trying to contact a federal marshal, but . . ."

"But what?"

"But maybe you can help me."

"I'm not a lawman, Mrs. Lake."

"I know, that, but you see that I have a problem. And you said you like to help people."

"Well . . ."

"Maybe you could just go to Hays and talk to the undertaker," she went on. "Perhaps he'd be scared of you."

"I suppose I could ride to Hays and ask some questions."

"*We* could ride," she said. "If you go, I'm going with you."

He couldn't see any reason to tell her no. And he had been in town for such a short time that he was surprised he had already gotten himself involved in somebody else's business.

"Very well, then," Clint said. "We'll leave first thing in the morning. I'll meet you in front of your store at eight."

"Wonderful!" she gushed. "You can't believe how grateful I am. Come, I'll walk you out."

He thought she meant out of the apartment, but she walked him down the stairs and to the front door. The young clerk stared at her, quite moon-eyed.

At the door he asked, "What about your store?"

"Thad can handle business until I get back."

"What about a buggy?" he asked.

"I don't need a buggy," she said. "I can ride, and I have a horse out back."

"In that case, I'll see you in the morning."

"I'll be ready," she promised.

Clint left, and she closed the door. As she turned and walked past the front desk the clerk asked, "Are you goin' away again, Sally?"

"Thad," she said, "close the store, come upstairs and take your pants off."

The young man rushed from behind the desk.

***

When Sally Lake got back to her apartment, she was feeling more positive than she had in days. Surely a man like the Gunsmith would be able to get something done. By the time Thad came rushing into the apartment, Sally was fully naked. The boy stopped short and stared at her full breasts and lovely skin. She could see by the bulge in his crotch that he was already excited.

"Get your pants off, boy!" she growled.

"Yes, Ma'am."

Sally, thirty-five, knew that the nineteen-year-old boy was quite in love with her. He couldn't wait for the time they spent together when her husband was away. This time, she had traveled with her spouse, so now

Thad was impatient, and shed his trousers and underwear quickly. In moments his young cock, long, hard sock was reaching out to her.

She walked to him, fell to her knees, and immediately took him into her mouth. She sucked him wetly. reaching around to dig her nails into his skinny butt. While he had a very nice penis, the rest of his body was skin and bones. She rarely took his shirt off, not wanting to see his mostly concave chest.

When she felt him begin to tremble, she released him from her mouth, stood, grasped his cock in her right hand and said, "Bedroom," leading him there.

"Come on, come," she said, impatiently. She climbed on the bed, laid on her back and spread her legs for him.

Without hesitating, the boy climbed atop her and drove his hard cock into her wet, steamy depths. Immediately, he started jamming himself in and out of her anxiously.

"Good God, Thad," she said, grabbing his hips to slow him, "take it easy. We have all night."

Chapter Five

When Clint headed for his hotel, he suddenly decided to make a detour to the sheriff's office. It was true Wilson had no jurisdiction in Hays, but the man might be able to tell Clint something helpful about the undertaker. When he reached the office, he found the door unlocked. Something told him to knock. After the second time, the door was opened by Zack Wilson, who appeared to have been sleeping.

"Adams," he said, rubbing his face. "Come on in."

Clint entered and found himself in a very small, messy office that looked as if the man had been living there for some time.

"I know what you're thinkin'," Wilson said.

"Doesn't a place to live come with the job?" Clint asked.

"I'm lucky they let me keep my badge and this office. They took the house back."

Wilson walked around his desk and sat.

"What's on your mind?"

"I'm heading for Hays tomorrow."

"What for?"

"I'm going to try to help Mrs. Lake."

"Why not?" Wilson asked. "She's a pretty widow."

"I don't like the idea of a crooked undertaker," Clint said. "Can you tell me anything about him?"

"Whataya wanna know?"

"How long's he been the undertaker in Hays?"

"A long time," Wilson said. "So long he's an institution there. Folks respect him, but mostly they fear him."

"They fear an undertaker? Why?"

"I think you'll find out when you get there."

"What's his name?"

"Jagger," Wilson said, "Charles Jagger."

"And who's the sheriff?"

"Dan Blakely," Wilson said. "He's been there about six years."

"What's he like?"

"He does his job."

"And how's he feel about Jagger?"

"The same as everyone else in town."

"I'm starting to really look forward to meeting this undertaker," Clint said.

"You'll find him interestin'," Wilson said. "He doesn't exactly look like an undertaker."

"What's he look like?"

"He dresses well, keeps himself neat and clean."

"How old is he?"

"That's hard to tell," Wilson said. "He could be fifty or eighty."

"He sounds like some character," Clint said.

"The only piece of advice I can give you is, don't underestimate him."

"Okay, Sheriff," Clint said. "Thanks for talking to me. Sorry to wake you."

"It don't matter," Wilson said, with a wave. "Good luck to you."

Clint left the office, feeling sorry for the man for having to live in the cramped office.

***

When Clint got back to the hotel, he stopped at the front desk.

"What can I do for you, sir?" the middle-aged desk clerk asked.

"You can prepare my bill," Clint said. "I'll be checking out in the morning."

"So soon?"

"My business here is finished," Clint said.

"Very well, sir," the clerk said. "Your bill will be ready by seven."

"Seven?"

"Yes, sir," the man said, "that's first thing in the mornin' for us."

"Does that go for the dining room, too?"

"Oh yes, sir."

"Good to know," Clint said. "I'll have breakfast before I leave town."

"See you in the mornin', sir," the clerk said.

Clint went up to his room.

***

After breakfast he walked to the livery to collect his Tobiano. When he rode over to the General Store, he found Sally Lake sitting in a chair out front. There was a good looking sorrel tied to the hitching post.

"What a nice horse," she said, as he dismounted.

"Good-morning, and thanks. This one yours?"

"She is," Sally said. "Her name's Lady."

There were a couple of sacks hanging from her saddle.

I packed light," she told him. "Everything we'll need is in these gunny sacks."

"That's the way I prefer to travel," he replied. "Are you ready to go?"

"All set."

"What about your store?"

"As I told you, Thad can handle it."

"He doesn't mind?" Clint asked.

"Why would he?"

"I got the feeling the young man has real feelings for you."

"That's silly," she said. "He was devoted to my husband, Charles. He's awfully happy to do whatever he can to help both of us."

"Then there's nothing keeping us from getting started," Clint said.

He helped her to mount up, climbed aboard Toby, and off they went.

Chapter Six

On the first night they camped at dusk, feeling no need to ride in the dark. Even though Sally was in a hurry to get there, she understood it was dangerous to ride at night.

As they stopped for the second night, Clint noticed that Sally was looking distressed.

"What's wrong?" he asked. "Having a change of heart?"

"N-no, it's not that," she said. "I've had this feeling all day that we're being followed."

"I have a pretty good sense about that," Clint said. "We'll camp here for the night, and I'll keep a sharp eye out."

"Okay."

They dismounted and while Clint took care of the horses, Sally proved herself very useful in building a fire, and making a meal for them, including a pot of coffee.

When they were seated around the campfire, eating bacon-and-beans, washing it down with coffee, Clint asked, "Still feel unsettled?"

"Well . . . I guess not, if you're sure nobody's behind us," she said.

"I'm sure," he said. "Besides, why would someone be following us?"

"Maybe because they're after you," she said. "Somebody in town could have recognized you."

"That's true," Clint said, "but if that was the case, I'd know it."

"What if they're ahead, waiting to bushwhack us?"

"I'd notice that, too."

"So, no one can ever shoot you from hiding?"

"If it's unplanned and they do it at a moment's notice so that I can't sense that they're there."

"You're pretty sure of yourself."

"I'm very sure," he said. "It's the only way I stay alive. And there's no reason anyone would spot us and suddenly decide to bushwhack us. We're just a man and a woman out riding."

"I'm curious," she said, "what if it's Indians?"

"The Indians are on reservations now," Clint said, "but just for the sake of argument, it would be harder for me to spot Indians. They have a way of blending in with the background."

"Have you fought Indians?"

"I have. Years ago I was a scout for the Army."

"I'm sure your reputation is quite bloated by the press, but you must have had a rather full life."

"I'm having a full life," he said. "It's not over, yet."

"I'll clean up and turn in," she said.

"Go ahead," Clint said. "I'll take care of all this."

As she rolled herself into her bedroll, Clint collected the plates and utensils. Since they weren't near a stream or water hole, he cleaned, using dirt. Then he made another pot of coffee and sat up for a while, having a few cups. He had certainly had better meals off the trail, but trail coffee was still his favorite. Nowhere else was it as black and strong.

He listened to the quiet, paid attention to Toby to see if he was reacting to anything. When he was sure no one was about, he turned in, himself.

***

The next two days and night of travelling were uneventful. She asked him more questions about his life and reputation, and he answered by giving her as few facts as possible. When he started asking questions about her life, she told him she was orphaned at a young age, went out at her own at twelve, worked a variety of jobs—including saloon girl but never whore. At fifteen she was working in a saloon, met Charles Lake, and married him.

"Just like that?" he asked. "Why?"

"Simple," she said. "He asked me, and promised he'd take care of me."

"Did he . . ."

"Rape me? Never. I had sex with him because I wanted him to be happy. You see, I wanted to be a good wife, and I believe I was, for twenty-years."

"How much older than you was he?"

"Thirty years."

"And when he died?"

"Sixty-five."

"Were you still having sex?"

"Oh, no," she said, "that stopped years ago when he wasn't able to. But I didn't mind. I still respected and took good care of him, cooked for him, kept house, worked in the store with him. Up to the day he died we were still happy."

"And now the store is yours."

"I don't want it," she said. "As soon as we get all this stuff settled in Hays, I'll go back to Kansas City and sell it."

"And then do what?"

She shrugged.

"I don't know," she said. "I'll have money, so maybe I'll see the world. I could meet some princes and kings in Europe, maybe have sex with some of them."

"Marry again?"

"Oh, I don't think so," she said. "At least, not for a lot of years. Maybe when I'm old I'll do what my husband did, marry someone a lot younger who can take care of me."

"Sounds like you've got it all worked out," he said.

He was surprised by how freely she talked about her sex life with her husband, and then what it might be like in the future. It almost made him curious enough to crawl into her bedroll with her some night, but he put that off. If it happened, it could happen in a more comfortable setting. For now, he simply wanted to help her get her husband's things back and nail the crooked undertaker.

Chapter Seven

On the sixth day they rode into Hays, sweaty and dirty.

"What will we do first?" she asked, as they rode in.

"I think a room, a meal and a bath, in that order," he said. He threw the bath in for her benefit.

"That sounds divine."

"Then tomorrow we can go and see the undertaker."

They rode to the Hays livery and left their horses in the hands of the hostler. Carrying their saddlebags, and Clint his rifle, he followed Sally to the Hays House Hotel.

"This was where I stayed with my husband," she explained.

"Are you sure you want to stay here?" he asked.

"It's the best hotel in town," she said. "I'll pay for the rooms."

"Whatever you say."

They checked in and got rooms that were across from each other. Before going up, Clint talked to the clerk about baths.

"We have a tub in the hotel the lady can use," the man said. "You can go across the street to the barber shop. He has several."

"Sounds good," Clint said.

They went up to their rooms, dropped off their saddlebags and came back down with a change of clothes.

"I'll see you after our baths, and we'll get something to eat," Clint said.

"That's fine."

Sally had an entire change of clothes, while Clint carried a fresh shirt across to the barber shop.

There was a man in one of the two barber chairs, and no one waiting.

"I'll be with you in a few minutes, sir," the barber said.

"Actually, I wanted to use one of your bathtubs."

"Oh, sure, go right ahead," the barber said. "In the back. It's fifty cents."

"That's fine."

"A haircut after?"

"No, thanks."

"Suit yourself."

The barber went back to the man in the chair, whose face was covered by a hot towel.

When Clint went into the back to use a tub, the shop door opened, and the hotel clerk entered.

"Where is he, Floyd?" he asked the barber.

"Who?"

"The man who just came in."

"He's in the back, takin' a bath. Why?"

"He just checked into the hotel."

"So?"

"He's Clint Adams, the Gunsmith."

The man in the chair pulled the towel from his face and looked at the clerk. His name was Gus Hedges, and he fancied himself a gun for hire.

"Are you sure, Sam?" he asked.

"That's how he signed in."

"As the Gunsmith?"

"No, as Clint Adams."

"Is he alone?"

"No, he checked in with a woman. They have separate rooms."

"Do you know who the woman is?"

"Sure do," the clerk said. "She was here a couple of weeks ago, when her husband died in bed."

"*That* woman?" the barber said.

"You better let Jagger know," the barber said. "And the sheriff."

"I don't care about some woman," Gus said. "Is the Gunsmith alone, otherwise?"

"Yep," the clerk said, "all alone."

"Get out of here before he comes back," the barber said.

"Right, but I'll tell Jagger and the sheriff, first."

"What's the woman doin' while he's here?" Sam asked.

"She's takin' a bath in the hotel."

"Okay," Floyd said, waving his scissors, "get outta here."

"Right."

As Sam left, Gus got out of the barber's chair.

"I ain't done," Floyd said.

"You are now," Gus said, grabbing his hat and leaving the shop.

That left Floyd alone to face the Gunsmith when he came out, and he wasn't comfortable with that, at all."

***

Clint filled one of the tubs with hot water. He had a choice of cold water, or first heating it on a stove, so he chose to heat it. He knew Sally would come out smelling sweet and clean, so he wanted to at least be clean for her.

When he was done, he dried off, donned his clean shirt and went out to the shop to pay the barber. He noticed that the man was very nervous.

"Fifty cents, you said?" Clint asked.

"Yessir!" the barber said. "If that's all right with you, sir."

"Hey, that's your price, right?" Clint asked. "That's fine."

He gave the man four bits.

"T-thank you, sir."

Clint noticed the man's hand shook when he took the money. The only reason he could think of for such a case of nerves was if the man knew who he was. He didn't seem to recognize him when he came in, so something must have happened while he was taking a bath.

"Did the desk clerk come across and tell you who I was?" he asked.

"Um, well, uh, yessir."

"And the fella in your chair, he knows, now?"

"Yessir."

"So it's going to get all over town, isn't it?" Clint asked.

"Um, that's very likely, sir."

Taking a nice, hot bath may not have been worth it after all.

Chapter Eight

"When Clint got back to the hotel, the clerk eyed him nervously as he walked across the lobby. At the second floor he knocked on Sally's door, even though he didn't expect her to be there. To his surprise, she opened it. In his experience, women took longer baths than that.

But as he expected, she smelled sweet and clean.

He told her the bad news, that the word would be getting around town that he was there.

"What's that going to mean, exactly?" she asked.

"I don't know, maybe nothing, maybe someone will get brave and challenge me."

"And you'll have to kill them?"

"If I can't talk them out of it," he said. "I probably should go and see the sheriff. Maybe he'll have a suggestion to keep it from happening."

"Like what?" she asked.

"Oh, he'll probably suggest strongly that I leave town."

"We've only just arrived."

"Then I guess we better not wait until tomorrow," Clint said. "Let's grab a meal, and then stop at the sheriff's office."

"And tell him exactly why we're here?"

"I think when he sees you, he'll figure it out. Right now, let's go get something to eat."

***

When Gus Hedges left the barber shop, he hurried to the sheriff's office. Sheriff Barkley looked up from his desk as Gus rushed in.

"What's your hurry?" Barkley asked.

"I've got news," Gus said. "The Gunsmith's in town."

"That's crazy," Barkley said. "What would the Gunsmith be doin' here?"

"You're gonna hear it from the clerk at the Hays House. Will you believe it then?"

"But why would the Gunsmith come here?"

"Well, apparently he's here with that woman whose husband died a couple of weeks ago."

"Sally Lake, from Kansas City?"

"If that's her name, yeah."

"If she's here with the Gunsmith, then she got him interested in her complaint against Jagger."

"Maybe the Gunsmith will kill 'im," Gus said. "That wouldn't be so bad."

"Sure, let Jagger hear you say that."

"Never mind that," Gus said. "This is my chance to get a reputation."

"You wanna go after Clint Adams? That's crazy!"

"I'm not talkin' about doin' it alone," Gus said. "I know a couple of my pals who'd be interested."

"Just hold off," Barkley said. "Let's find out what he wants in Hays, first."

"How you gonna find that out?"

"Easy," Sheriff Barkley said. "I'm gonna ask 'im."

"Just like that?"

"Why not?" Barkley said. "I'm the law, ain't I?"

"You want some backup. I know at least three other guns—"

"I don't want you or your friends around me," Barkley said. "Just hold back before you do somethin' stupid, Gus. Go talk to your friends and tell them the same thing."

"Well, all right, but don't go tryin' to take him yourself."

"I'm gonna talk with him," Barkley said. "Just talk. Just make yourself scarce and wait to hear from me. Now go!"

***

Sally and Clint found a café that was doing a good enough business to indicate the food was probably good. They were seated at a back table and ordered the beef stew special from the blackboard on the wall.

When they had bowls of stew and mugs of beer in front of them, they continued to discuss their plans.

"If we got to the sheriff first, won't he warn the undertaker?" she asked.

"If they're in on it together, probably," Clint said. "If he does, that will tell us something."

"Why can't the sheriff just get me back my husband's things?" she asked, frustrated. "Then we wouldn't have to go through all of this."

"I might be able to talk some sense into the man," Clint suggested.

"You said the sheriff in Kansas City said the folks around here are afraid of this Jagger."

"That's what he told me."

"Well, maybe you can make them more afraid of you," she said.

"I don't like scaring people."

"But aren't they afraid when you just ride into a town?" she asked.

"Sometimes," he said, "but it's really not something I look forward to. I'd rather be ignored."

"You certainly don't sound like a man with a big reputation," she said. "I thought you—they—wanted the attention."

"Not when the attention comes with flying lead," he said.

"Then why live that life?"

"Well," he said, "you don't start out that way, and then later, it becomes too late to change. So . . ."

"You can't settle down?" she asked. "Live on a farm or a ranch somewhere?"

"That's not something they're going to let me do," he told her. "No matter how hard I try."

They finished their stew, Sally paid the bill, and they left the café to go in search of the sheriff's office."

Chapter Nine

It only took a three street walk to find the lawman's office. Even from the front it looked larger than Sheriff Wilson's office in Kansas City.

"I'm going to guess that Hays doesn't have a modern police department," Clint said, as they approached.

"No," Sally said. "I only talked with the sheriff, and only at the undertakers, or my hotel. Never here."

They stepped up onto the boardwalk and opened the door. Clint let Sally go in first.

"You're back," the sheriff said. He was seated behind his desk and did not bother to stand. He was in his fifties, a little thick, but he looked like a man able to do his job. "And you brought a friend."

"Come on, Sheriff," Clint said. "You already know who I am."

"Yes, I do," Barkley said. "It's my job to know. What can I do for you?"

"I understand your undertaker's a crook."

"Well now," Barkley said, "that's not somethin' that's ever been proven."

"Maybe while I'm here, I can manage to do that," Clint said.

"And what d'ya want from me?"

"I just wanted to let you know I'm here, and I'm not looking for trouble."

"Calling our undertaker crooked is not looking for trouble?" Barkley said.

"Not until I do it to his face, I suppose," Clint said. "But I also wanted you to tell me if you knew of anyone in town who was going to make the mistake of trying me."

"Well, now that you mention it, there might be a couple of boys who think they're gunnies."

"Then maybe you could warn them to stay away from me," Clint said, "With a little luck, we'll only be here a day or two."

"Why don't you tell me what exactly you think you're gonna accomplish?"

"That's simple," Clint said. "We want Mrs. Lake's husband's possessions, as well as his remains."

"I don't see a problem with you gettin' his body back," Sheriff Barkley said. "You're free to dig it up and take it with you."

"And my husband's things?" she demanded.

"The undertaker claims he returned them all to you," Barkley said.

"He's lying," she said. "He stole them."

"And I told you the first time you were here, Ma'am, you can't prove that."

"Let's see what happens when I try," Clint suggested.

"Mr. Adams," the sheriff said, "if you threaten our undertaker—or anyone, for that matter—with your gun, I'm afraid I'll have to lock you up."

"How many deputies do you have?"

"How many would I need?" Barkley asked.

He and Clint both laughed, leading Sally to stare at them, uncomprehendingly.

"Thanks for making contact with me, Adams," Barkley said. "I hope you can accomplish what you want without too much—"

"—blood?" Clint asked.

"—difficulty." He looked at Sally. "Ma'am, again, I'm sorry for your loss."

"Thank you, Sheriff," she said. "That's not very comforting but thank you."

She and Clint left the office.

"You two were laughing like old friends," she said. "I don't get it."

"We recognized each other."

"You knew each other before?"

"Not personally," Clint said, "but we know each other's type."

"What type is that?"

"The type who usually gets the job done."

"He didn't strike me as that type the last time I was here," she pointed out.

"He does what he can, Sally, within the letter of the law. "I think if we can prove that the undertaker's a crook, the sheriff might take some action."

"I hope so."

"Let's see what we can find out tomorrow."

They headed back to the hotel for the night.

Chapter Ten

Clint and Sally went to their own rooms for the night. But when there was a knock at his door, Clint wasn't surprised. He thought all of Sally's talk about her sex life was leading up to something.

When he opened the door, she was standing in the hall wearing a robe and holding a bottle of whiskey and two glasses.

"I got these from the night clerk," she said, brandishing them.

"Come on in," he said.

As she entered, he closed the door behind her and made sure it was locked. There were two chairs in the room, but she chose to sit on the bed. As he sat next to her, she handed him a glass, and then poured whiskey into each.

"Here's to a pleasant night of getting to know one another," she said.

"We've been together a week," he said. "I think we know each other pretty well."

"We know each other hardly at all," she told him, "but we're going to fix that."

He sipped his whiskey and watched as she stood and shed the robe. It fell to the floor around her ankles. She was a well-built lady who had maintained most of her body's vitality through her thirties. She put one hand around to the back of his head and pulled him to her full bosom.

"It's been a long time for me," she said, as he nuzzled her nipples.

"You said you had sex with your husband."

"Yes," she said, "but not for years."

"And you've gone without since then?"

"Not without," she said, "exactly. But it's been a long time since I've been with a real man."

She put her arms around his neck and kissed him deeply.

"Do you mind?" she asked. "I don't know if we'll get this opportunity again."

"You were talking about my reputation," he said. "You're not exactly what I expected from a recent widow."

"I told you I was married a long time, and we treated each other right. I never said we were in love, Clint."

"No, you didn't."

She settled back on her heels and started unbuttoning his shirt . . .

***

Sheriff Barkley left his office soon after Clint and Sally did. He stood in front of his office and made sure they were nowhere in sight, then began walking. He turned down a side street and walked until he reached a building with one word over the door. It said:

UNDERTAKER.

He entered.

An older man came from a back room. He could have been anywhere from fifty to eighty. Barkley knew the man's true age. He also knew how expensive the suit of clothes he wore was. This undertaker was wealthier than any other he had ever met. And there were no coffins in sight. They were all in the back, and extremely well made, rather than the flimsy boxes most undertakers dealt with.

Charles Jagger was unlike any other undertaker Sheriff Barkley had seen in all his years of being a lawman throughout the West.

"Sheriff," Jagger said, "what brings you here?"

"Sally Lake is back in town."

"What does she want?"

"I think you know."

"She still thinks I l have her husband's effects?"

"She does, and she wants his body."

"Let her have that."

"She won't take that and just leave," Barkley said. "She still wants more."

"Can't you take care of her?"

"She's not alone."

"Oh? Did she bring another lawman with her? One who has no jurisdiction?"

"Not a lawman," Barkley said.

"Then who?"

"She has Clint Adams with her," the sheriff said.

"What?"

"The Gunsmith."

"I know who Clint Adams is," Jagger said. "What's he doin' here?"

"I guess he wants to help 'er."

"So he's not wearin' a badge?" Jagger asked.

"No," Barkley said, "no badge."

"Is he coming here?"

"Probably not tonight."

"Good," Jagger said. "I'm going home. If he comes there, he won't like the reception he gets."

"Good luck," the lawman said, and turned to leave.

"What's your part going to be in all this?" Jagger asked Sheriff Barkley.

"I'll do my job," Barkley said, and left.

Jagger knew the lawman had not chosen a side, but he was a smart man, and the undertaker felt sure he would pick the right one, when it came right down to it.

After the sheriff left, Jagger called his assistant, Ivan, out from the back.

"Yes, Mr. Jagger?" the small man asked.

"Ivan, tomorrow we're going to have a visitor," Jagger said. "This is what I want you to do . . ."

***

When Sally had Clint completely nude and his cock was hard and full, she knew she had made the right choice to come to his room. She saw how much time she had been wasting with young Thad, now that she had a real man.

She pushed Clint down on his back and climbed atop him. There would be time to explore his body later. At the moment she just wanted that cock deep inside her.

She lifted her butt and came down on him, brutally taking him inside. Once he was there, she started riding up and down on him, grunting every time she came down.

Clint watched as her breasts bounced in front of him, and finally reached for them, filling his hands with their weight. She continued to work his penis in-and-out, in-

and-out. She was finally overcome by her pleasure. Her body trembled, and fell over him, her breasts crushed to his chest, his cock still inside her.

Clint put his hands on her hips and rolled her off him. As his penis came free, it glistened with her juices. Still hard, he slid atop her, took a leg in each hand, spread her wide and drove himself into her once again. This time she screamed . . .

***

She laid with her head on his chest, trying to catch her breath. Never before had a man exhausted her that way. Her husband was too old, and Thad was too young.

"My God," she whispered.

"You said it," he agreed, also breathing hard.

"I feel like I've wasted most of my life," she said. "First with my older husband, and then . . . well . . ."

"You don't have to explain," he said. "You're a woman who deserved more."

"Yes," she said.

"But now you've got whatever money your husband left you, and the business," he told her. "You can do what you want with whoever you want."

"I think," she said, sliding her hand down to grasp his cock, "you know who I want now."

"We've got all night," he said, "and in the morning, we'll do what we came here to do."

She stroked his cock until it was good and hard again, and then put it to good use . . .

***

When Clint pressed his face to her crotch and worked on her with his mouth and tongue, she gasped aloud. He held her down while she bucked and struggled and kept her there until her struggles ceased and she collapsed.

Breathing hard she gasped, "No man . . . had ever done . . . that to me before."

"It seems you have wasted a lot of your time," he remarked. "Luckily you're young enough to make up for that wasted time."

"God," she said, grabbing him, "let's make up for as much of it as we can tonight!"

And they did . . . until they were finally able to fall asleep in each other's arms . . .

Chapter Eleven

The next morning, after breakfast, Clint and Sally walked to the undertaker's office and found the door unlocked. As they entered, a little man about sixty came out from the back. He wore a long, leather apron over his clothes, and his hands were dirty. Clint assumed this man built the coffins for the undertaker.

"Yes, sir?" the man said. "Can I help you?"

"I'm looking for the undertaker, Mr. Jagger."

"I'm afraid Mr. Jagger isn't here, today."

"Then where is he?" Sally asked. "We need to talk to him."

"He's at home."

"Where's that?"

"About ten miles north of town," the man said. "He told me he'd be there all day."

Clint looked at Sally.

"Have you ever been there?"

"No," she said, "I didn't even know he had a home outside of town."

"All right," Clint said, and looked at the man, "we'll go there and speak to him."

"Mr. Jagger has a lot of men there," the little man said.

"What's an undertaker need with a lot of men?" Clint asked.

"Oh, Mr. Jagger is much more than just an undertaker," the man said. "He owns lots of businesses in town."

"And his home," Clint asked, "is it a ranch?"

"Yes, sir, the largest ranch in the area."

"Built with money he stole, I'll bet," Sally said.

"What?" the little man said. "Oh, no, Mr. Jagger is very fair in his dealings."

Clint assumed Jagger knew they would be coming, so he told this little man what to say.

"What's your name?" he asked.

"Ivan."

"What do you do?"

"I build the coffins and prepare the bodies for burial."

"And what does Jagger do?"

"Why . . . he owns the place."

"I mean, what does he do himself, with his own hands?" Clint explained.

"For years he did everything himself, but when he became an important man he hired me," Ivan explained.

"What's in the back, Ivan?" Clint asked.

"My workshop."

"Can we see it?"

"Well . . . sure, I don't see why not. Follow me."

Ivan went through the door into the back.

"Why do we want to see his workshop?" Sally asked.

"You just tell me if you see anything back there that's familiar."

"Ah, okay."

They went through the door after Ivan.

***

Charles Jagger ate breakfast at a large table in the dining room of his home.

His cook brought him more coffee and asked, "Anything else, sir?" The woman was heavyset, in her fifties, and had been working for him for more than a dozen years.

"No, nothing else, Martha," he said, while she poured. "You can clean up. The flapjacks were excellent, as usual, as well as the bacon. Perfect!"

"Thank you, sir."

"Leave the pot," he said. "I'm expecting some of the men."

"Yessir."

She grabbed as many of the plates as she could and carried them to the kitchen. Jagger heard his front door open, and then three of his men entered the dining room. They were all wearing holstered pistols.

"It's about time," he said.

"You didn't say an exact time, boss," one man said. "Just mornin'."

"Fine, fine," Jagger said. "Here's what's happening. A man is coming to see me this morning. I want the three of you to be ready to kill him, if need be."

"Sure, boss," the first man sad. "Uh, how do we know if we're supposed to do it?"

"I'll let you know," Jagger said. "I won't want it done on my property."

"Do ya want him killed a certain way?" another man asked.

"Shot," Jagger said, "I'll want him shot. That way, when he's found, it won't be a surprise to anyone."

"Why not?" the first man asked.

"Because the man I'm talking about is Clint Adams, the Gunsmith."

"The Gunsmith?" the third man snapped in surprise.

"Is that a problem?" Jagger asked. "You'll all be well paid once it's done."

"And you want just the three of us to do it?" the second man asked.

"I can get three others, if you like, and pay them, instead. I don't want a lot of people knowing about this."

"That's okay, boss," the first man said. "We'll do it. There's no problem."

"Okay," Jagger said. "I want one of you watching the house at all times. You'll see him arrive."

"How will we know it's him?"

"You'll know," Jagger said. "He'll probably have a woman with him. After he leaves, I'll come out on the porch and wave. You'll know. Now go."

The three men filed out.

Chapter Twelve

Clint and Sally went to the livery and saddled their horses.

"How are we going to do this?" Sally asked.

"We're going to ride out there and talk to the man," Clint answered.

"Are you going to threaten him?"

"I haven't made up my mind yet," Clint told her.

"I'd rather you just tell him if he doesn't give back my husband's things, you'll kill him."

"You think he'll believe that?"

"Why not?" Sally asked. "You're the Gunsmith."

"This doesn't sound like a man who scares easily," Clint observed.

"Then shoot off a finger," she suggested. "That would scare most people."

"Sally," Clint said, "if I can, I'm going to get back your belongings without shooting anybody. Tell me that's not good enough, and I'll quit right now."

"No, no," she said frustrated, "do it your way."

"Okay, then," Clint said, "let's ride on out there."

They both mounted up and rode their horses out of the livery.

***

When they came within sight of the ranch, they reined their horses in and stared.

"Can this be it?" Sally wondered. "It's huge. We're probably already on his land."

"We might have been on his land for some time," Clint said. "Apparently, this undertaker, Jagger, is very wealthy."

"Why would a wealthy man steal from the dead?" Sally asked.

"Maybe," Clint said, "that's how he became wealthy, and that's how he stays that way."

"But the things he stole from my husband would mean so little to a man like that."

"Then it may not be what he steals," Clint said, "as much as the stealing itself."

"You mean he just likes to do it?"

"Some men get a thrill from stealing, even small things."

"I find that hard to understand."

"Maybe we can get him to explain it to you," Clint said. "Let's go."

They urged their horses forward and rode up to the large two-story house. It was built in the fashion of large, Southern mansions, with thick white columns.

Clint looked around, didn't see anyone.

"Where is everyone?" he wondered aloud. "The place looks deserted, not like a working ranch, at all."

"Couldn't the men be away?" she asked. "Like on a trail drive, or rounding up the stock?"

"Could be," Clint said, "but this ground doesn't look well-trod."

He dismounted, and helped Sally down from her horse, then tied both mounts off. They went up the steps to the front door and knocked. A thick-set woman wearing an apron answered it.

"Yes?"

"We're here to see Mr. Jagger," Clint said.

"Can I tell him why?" she asked.

"To get back what he stole," Sally said.

The woman looked shocked. "What?"

"Never mind," Clint said. "Just tell him Mrs. Lake is here about her husband's body."

"I'll tell 'im," she said, and closed the door.

"I'm sorry," Sally said. "I just hate that he's rich and has servants."

"She looks like his cook, but I get your point. Just let me do most of the talking."

"All right," she said, "I'll try."

When the door opened the woman said, "He has agreed to see you."

"Thank you."

"But you'll have to go around back." she said.

"We can't go in the front?"

"He's actually not in the house."

"Where is he?" Clint asked.

"He has a workshop in the back," she said. "You'll see it when you go around."

She slammed the door before Clint could say another word.

Chapter Thirteen

Clint and Sally walked around the house and found a smaller structure. They walked to the door, which was open, and peered in. It was obviously a workshop, loaded with tools and wood. In the center of the room was a man with his sleeves rolled up, revealing muscular forearms. He looked like a healthy physical specimen, but when Clint saw his face, he knew what Sheriff Wilson was talking about. The man could have been anywhere from fifty to eighty. He had a head of long, white hair with a shiny pink scalp showing through, and a white beard.

"Mr. Adams," he said, straightening from the workbench he had been bent over, "and Mrs. Lake. Welcome to my shop."

"Workshop?" Clint asked. "I don't see any coffins."

"Oh, Ivan makes the coffins in town," Jagger said. "Out here I make furniture."

Clint looked around again, this time noticing the benches and chests of drawers.

"It looks like you do nice work," Clint said.

"Thank you. Excuse me for not shaking hands, but I've been working all morning. I like to get an early start."

He put down the hammer he had been holding, picked up a rag and wiped his hands with it.

"What can I do for you?"

"I think you know why we're here, Mr. Jagger," Sally said.

"I'm afraid I don't, Mrs. Lake."

"I want my husband's belongings."

"Oh, that again?" the undertaker asked. "I thought we had settled that already."

"Apparently," Clint said, "nothing's been settled."

Jagger stopped wiping his hands and tossed the rag away, then put his hands on his hips.

"I'm afraid I don't understand—"

"Yes, you do, you thief!" Sally shouted.

"Mr. Adams," Jagger said, calmly, "if you would control your lady friend—"

"She's not my lady friend," Clint said, "she's a widow who believes she's been taken advantage of, and I want to help her."

"Well, that's very noble of you, sir, but I don't know what I can do—"

Sally started to speak again, but Clint put his hand on her shoulder.

"Mr. Jagger, you can start by giving her husband's body to her so she can take it home and bury him."

"That's not a problem, Mr. Adams," Jagger said. "As soon as I get back to town I'll have my assistant, Ivan, take care of that. I'll even supply a wagon for the ride home."

"And since you claim to have no knowledge of her husband's belongings going missing, perhaps you can suggest something that might have happened to them.

"I haven't got the faintest idea, unless . . ."

"Unless what?" Clint asked.

"Unless some of his belongings were buried with him by mistake."

"Would you make a mistake like that," Clint asked, "A man with your experience?"

"Not me," Jagger said, "but Ivan is getting older . . ."

"So your assistant might have made a mistake."

"It's possible," Jagger said, "But I'm afraid to find out for sure. We would not only have to dig up the body but open the coffin and have a look inside. Tell me, what sort of belongings are we talking about?"

"Some jewelry," Clint said. "A watch, a stick pin—"

"Yes," Jagger said, "things of that nature could be overlooked. It will take me some time to clean up, then I can ride into town and look into this."

"And you couldn't do this the last time the lady was here?" Clint asked.

Jagger looked as if he was going to speak but stopped abruptly. The next time he spoke he lowered his voice.

"Mr. Adams," he said, "if we could speak in private—"

"How dare you—" Sally started, but Clint silenced her again.

"Let me talk to Mr. Jagger, Sally," he said. "Just step outside a minute."

Reluctantly, Sally obeyed.

"What were you going to say that you didn't want the lady to hear?" Clint asked.

"Well, when she was here last, she was very distraught. I mean, after all, her husband had died quite suddenly. I thought, in her condition, that she might have lost a few things and decided it was easier to blame me."

"When I met Mrs. Lake in Kansas City, she was quite calm, and convinced that the items had disappeared here, in Hays."

"Well," Jagger replied, "as I already said, I'm willing to dig the body up and we can have a look. You're welcome to wait for me, and we can ride to town together."

"That suits us," Clint said.

"Excellent," Jagger said. "You can wait in my living room, and I'll offer you refreshments."

"I don't think refreshments will be necessary," Clint said, "but we're willing to wait."

"Please," Jagger said, "come with me . . ."

***

Jagger's three men were waiting and watching from just inside the barn for a signal from their boss.

"How we gonna do this?" the second man asked.

"We'll follow Adams until him and the woman are away from the house," the leader of the three said, "and then we'll take 'im."

"Are we gonna ambush 'im?" the third man asked.

"You wanna go face-to-face with the Gunsmith?" the leader asked.

Chapter Fourteen

When Clint Adams and Sally Lake came back around the house to their horses, the men in the barn were ready to do their job. All they needed was a signal from Jagger.

Clint and Sally mounted up and rode away from the house. They had decided to meet Jagger there.

"Get the horses ready," the first man said. "We should get a signal any minute."

Sure enough, when Clint and Sally were out of sight, Charles Jagger came out the front door. However, he stood on the top step and waved the three men off, rather violently.

"What's goin' on?" the second man asked.

"I don't know," the first man said. "He's wavin' us off."

"Are you sure?" the third man asked.

The first man said. "Stay here. Lemme find out what's goin' on."

He left the barn and ran over to the house. When he got to the bottom step he stopped.

"What's goin' on, boss?" he asked.

"What part of this signal don't you understand?" Jagger asked.

"So you don't want us to kill 'im?"

"Very good," Jagger said. "You figured it out."

"But . . . why?"

"I've changed my mind," Jagger said. "I'm going to handle it another way. But I want you and the other two to stay ready, in case I change my mind again. Got it?"

"I guess so."

"I'm getting dressed and heading into town," Jagger said. "I want you to come with me, and the others to stay here. But stay ready."

"Got it."

"Then go and tell them to meet me back here with my carriage."

"Yes, sir."

The man turned and ran back to the barn.

***

As Clint and Sally rode away from the house, she asked, "What was that all about? I thought you were gonna scare him."

"I never said that. I said I was going to talk with him."

"And what good did that do?"

"Well, you're getting your husband's body back," Clint said. "That's one thing."

"But not the important thing," Sally said.

"It's a start," Clint said. "And we have him coming back to town."

"What's that going to accomplish?"

"I want him to lie to my face and try to blame it all on his assistant."

"Then what?"

"Then maybe we can get Ivan to talk."

"You think he'd give his boss away?"

"We can hope," Clint said. "That would be the easiest way to go."

"And the hard way?"

"There's still time to scare somebody."

"Is that the only reason we're riding back to town?"

"There were three men in the barn, waiting for us to come out," Clint told her.

"You can handle three men, can't you?"

"Let me put it this way," Clint replied. "There were three men that I know of."

"So you were afraid of getting killed?"

"I was concerned," Clint said, "if shooting started, you'd get killed. I want you back in town and safe if it comes to gunplay."

"I suppose I should be grateful for your concern."

"Sally," Clint said, "I want you to be alive when I get your property back."

"Okay, then," she said. "What are we gonna do when we get back?"

"We're going to get a drink and wait for Jagger to show. Then I suppose I'll go to his shop."

"You'll go?" she asked. "What about me?"

"Like I said, I want you safe. If Jagger had men at his house ready to shoot, chances are he'll have some there, too."

"So where will I be?"

"At the hotel."

"In my room, cowering?"

"In a front window," Clint said, "with a rifle."

"Nice try, but the undertaker's shop is off the main street, so I won't be able to see anything."

"You'll see what happens when he rides in," Clint said. "And when he and I head for his shop, you'll see if anyone follows."

"Ah," Sally said, "and then I'll follow."

"Right."

"What makes you think I can handle a gun?" she asked.

"There's a rifle in your saddle scabbard," he said. "It's not there for show, I hope."

"No," she confirmed, "I can shoot. I learned long ago, before I was married. I haven't forgotten."

"Good," Clint said. "The only important thing for you to remember is, don't shoot until I do."

"Got it."

That satisfied her, and they rode the rest of the way in silence.

***

When they got into town, Sally asked, "Has anybody been behind us?"

"No," Clint said. "If he has men they're already here."

"When do you think he'll get here?"

"I give him an hour," Clint said. "That's time to take care of our horses, have a drink, and get into position."

"I like the drink part," Sally said.

Chapter Fifteen

Before leaving their mounts at the livery, Clint took his Colt New Line from his saddlebag and tucked it into his belt at the small of his back. Then he took his rifle from his saddle. That done, he and Sally went to the closest saloon. It was small, hosting only a few drinkers, and had one saloon girl who looked as bored as the bartender. It was called The End of the Trail Saloon.

"Why such a long name for a small saloon?" Sally wondered.

"Well, look at it," Clint said. "It looks like the end of the trail."

They walked to the bar. No one gave them a look, as Sally's hair was tucked up under her hat, and her trail clothes were laden with trail dust.

"You in the right place?" the bartender asked.

"I think so," Clint said. "Two beers."

"Mugs or bottles?"

Clint gave the place another going over, and said, "Bottles."

"Why bottles?" Sally asked.

"I don't think we want to drink out of glasses here," he answered.

"Good point."

The bartender brought the beers and set them down.

"Two bits," he said.

Clint paid him.

"Mind if I ask you something?" Clint said.

"Sure, go ahead."

"Do you know the town undertaker?"

"Jagger?" the bartender said. "Everybody knows 'im."

"What can you tell me about him?" Clint asked.

"You don't wanna cross 'im."

"Why not?"

"Well," the bartender said, "you know how the undertaker buries ya after you die?"

"Yeah."

"Jagger does it the other way around," the barman said. "If you cross him, you end up dead and he buries ya."

"Are you serious?" Sally asked.

"Real serious, Ma'am."

"So you're saying he kills people?"

"I'm sayin' if you cross him, you die," the bartender said. "I didn't say he'd kill you himself. Somehow, you'd just die."

"Is that why people in town are afraid of him?"

"That's it," the bartender said. "He's downright creepy. Ask anybody."

Clint looked around at the sparse assemblage of men, and the girl leaning on the bar.

"Anybody else know anything about the undertaker, Mr. Jagger?" he asked, aloud.

Nobody answered until one man said, "We don't, none of us wanna know anythin' about him, Mister."

"He's supposed to bury people," the young girl said, "but he makes 'em die."

Clint moved down the bar to stand next to the girl in the yellow dress. She was filing her nails with great concentration and didn't even look at him.

"And how does he do that?"

She shrugged and said, "Nobody knows."

"How often has this happened?"

"Enough to make it creepy, like Al said."

Clint looked at the bartender again.

"Come on, how do they die?"

"Ain't got a mark on 'em," Al said, "but they're dead."

"And he buries them?"

"Yep."

"And what happens to their belongings?"

"Damned if I know."

"What about you?" Clint asked the girl.

This time she looked at him and liked what she saw. She stopped working on her nails.

"I don't rightly know, handsome," she said, "but why don't we go up to my room and talk about it?"

Sally moved up next to Clint and said to the girl, "Thanks for the invitation, but he's busy."

"Sorry, sweetie," the girl said, "I didn't know you was a girl."

"If you don't mind," Sally said, "I'm a woman. Come on, Clint!" She yanked his left arm.

"Thanks for the information," he said, "and the beer."

Outside the saloon Sally asked, "What was that all about?"

"Seems more may be going on here than meets the eye," Clint said. "You said your husband was dead when you woke up? Not a mark on him?"

"You mean . . ."

"Did your husband have a run-in with Jagger?"

"I don't see how," she said. "We only just arrived in town. We had a meal, went to our room and turned in."

"Did he get up and go out during the night?"

"If he did, he did it without waking me up."

Clint rubbed his jaw.

"Somehow, Jagger's killing people without leaving a mark on them," Clint said, "and stealing their belongings. I wonder what the families think?"

"He's getting away with it by scaring people," Sally said.

"I've got to get some names and then talk to the families."

"Where are you going to get the names?"

"Either from the sheriff, or the local newspaper."

"Which do we try first?" she asked.

"The sheriff didn't seem too helpful, the first time," Clint said. "Let's go talk to a newspaper editor."

"What about Jagger?" she asked. "He's on his way to town?"

"I'm sure he'll wait," Clint said. "He'll want to resolve this with as little attention as possible, if everything we've heard is true."

"And we're pretty damn sure it is, huh?" she asked.

"Yeah," Clint said, "pretty damn sure."

Chapter Sixteen

The local newspaper was called *The Hays Gazette*. They found the office on the main street, with the name of the paper filling the large front window.

"Do me a favor, Sally," Clint said. "When we go in there—"

"—let you do the talking."

Clint opened the door and let Sally go first. The press was quiet, but a man wearing a floor length white apron was standing at it, fiddling. The man looked up from the press at the two of them.

"What's on your mind?" he asked.

"We'd like to talk to the editor. Is that you?"

"Naw, he's in the office. His name's Mike Shane. Back room."

"Thanks."

Clint took Sally's elbow and pushed her ahead of him. They went down a long hallway to a closed door that said EDITOR on it. Clint knocked.

"Yeah, come on in," a man said in a sour tone.

When Clint and Sally entered, the man stood up from his desk, looking Sally over.

"Who're you hidin' from lady?" he asked.

Sally took off her hat and let her hair fall.

"Not hiding from anybody, Mister."

"Are you Shane, the editor?"

"That's me." Shane was a sad looking man who might have had many reasons for being sour. But he looked Sally up and down with real interest.

"Who're you?" he asked Clint, still staring at Sally.

"This is Sally Lake," Clint said. "I'm Clint Adams,"

That got Shane's attention.

"The Gunsmith? Whataya doin' in Hays?"

"I'm interested in Charles Jagger," Clint said.

"That's a dangerous man to be interested in."

"What can you tell me about him?"

"He's not somebody you wanna get involved with," he said.

"That's what I heard." Clint said.

"What do you want from me?"

"You're going to help me."

"Do what?"

"Prove Jagger's a crook," Clint said.

"A lot of people know that, already."

"And nobody does anything about it?"

"Some have tried."

"And what happened?"

"You ain't been listenin', friend. They're all dead."

"Why hasn't anybody sent for a U.S. Marshal?" Clint asked.

"Nobody wants to get on Jagger's bad side," Shane said.

"Why don't you use your power of the press against him?" Clint asked.

"Yeah," Shane said, "like I want to wake up dead one mornin'."

"Well, thanks very much, Mr. Shane," Clint said, sarcastically, "you've been a very big help."

"Hey," Shane said, "I'm still alive and I'm stayin' that way."

Clint and Sally walked out.

***

"The sheriff next?" Sally asked.

"I don't think he's going to be much help. I think we should go to Jagger next."

"Do you suspect he's in town by now?"

"We can go and check his shop," Clint said. "If he's not there yet, we can wait and talk with Ivan."

"What are you going to get from him?" she asked. "He works for the man."

"It sounds like he does all the work," Clint pointed out. "Maybe he's fed up and he'll give us something."

She took a deep breath and said, "Yeah, okay, let's give it a try."

They walked a short distance and turned on the side street the undertaker's shop was on.

***

While Clint and Sally were in with the newspaper editor, the undertaker, Jagger, drove his rig into town. Riding alongside him was one man named Rance. Jagger didn't bother looking around for Clint Adams but drove directly to his shop. He pulled his rig around back and entered through the workshop. Rance came in behind him but stepped to one side to await orders. Ivan was at work on a casket.

"Ivan!" he snapped. "Come with me."

"Sure, boss."

Jagger looked at Rance and said, "Stay here."

"Right, boss."

Ivan followed Jagger into the front of the shop.

"How many guests do we have?" Jagger asked him.

"Four."

"And valuables?"

"None."

That was just as well, with Clint Adams poking his nose in. Jagger had changed his mind about having

Adams killed from ambush. Everybody knew that Wild Bill Hickok was killed that way in Deadwood. He didn't want Hays to become that kind of famous town.

"The Gunsmith was out at my place this morning," Jagger told Ivan. "Now he's coming here to talk to you."

"Talk to me?" Ivan asked. "Why would he wanna talk to me, boss?"

"To see what you can tell 'im about me."

"I swear, boss," Ivan said, quickly, "I got nothin' to tell 'im!"

"I know that, Ivan," Jagger said. "I just want it to look like we're on the up-and-up. I don't want to hide nothin' from him."

"We got nothin' to hide, boss," Ivan said. "At least, not today."

Chapter Seventeen

"Change of plan," Clint said, as they walked. "Instead of in a hotel window, I want you with me."

"With a rifle?"

"No," Clint said, "with this." He took his Colt New Line from the back of his belt and passed it to her. He didn't want to be carrying saddlebags around if he was going to have to move fast. "Can you use it?"

"I can use it," she said, tucking it into her belt.

"I'll have to take your word for it, because I don't have time to test you."

"I can shoot," she said, again. "I told you, I was on my own at an early age. I learned how to take care of myself."

"You've been married a long time," Clint said.

"I kept in practice."

"All right. Take your shirt out of your belt. I want the gun hidden."

"She pulled her shirttail out and it covered the weapon. Only someone like Clint, who knew guns, would know it was there.

"Don't pull it out and shoot unless I do."

"Right."

As they approached the undertaker's shop, there was movement inside.

"I think he's there," Clint said.

"You know," she said, "I'd just as soon walk in and shoot him."

"You might get satisfaction from that, but that's all," Clint said. "Stick to the plan."

"Right."

Clint wasn't comfortable with Sally watching his back, but he had no choice. This had developed into a bad situation pretty quick. He wasn't dealing with your run-of-the-mill undertaker.

They stepped up onto the boardwalk and through the open door. The movement Clint had seen was Jagger and Ivan. Both men turned to face him.

"Mr. Adams," Jagger said. "Come in. This is Ivan. Ivan, this is Mr. Adams and Mrs. Lake."

"We met," Clint said. "But we didn't talk very long."

"Well, then," Jagger said, "go ahead and talk. I can do some work in the back."

Jagger stepped into the backroom. Rance started to move, but the undertaker waved at him to stay still. The undertaker stood just inside the door, so he could hear clearly.

***

"Let's step outside, Ivan," Clint said, assuming Jagger was eavesdropping.

"Uh, sure."

Clint and Ivan stepped outside, and Sally followed. Clint noticed she looked nervous, and hoped she wouldn't do anything rash.

As he started to stroll, Ivan went along. Sally stayed outside the shop.

"What's on your mind, Mr. Adams?" Ivan asked.

"I think you know, Ivan," Clint said. "Out of everyone in town, you're the one who knows what's really going on."

"Whataya mean?"

"Come on," Clint said, "Jagger's got everyone else buffaloed, but you're not afraid of him."

"You're wrong about that," Ivan said. "He terrifies me. So if you think I'm gonna talk against him, you're wrong."

"But he's breaking the law, Ivan," Clint said, "and that means you are, too."

"Nobody's ever proved that," the smaller man said.

"How long have you worked for him?" Clint asked.

"Twelve years or so."

"You must know him well."

"Not really," Ivan said. "We only see each other here at the shop."

"You've never been to his house?"

"No. We ain't friends. I work for him."

"That's all?"

"Yeah."

"What did he tell you to tell me?" Clint asked.

"Nothin'."

"Tell me nothing?"

"No, no," Ivan said, "I mean he just told me to answer your questions, but he didn't tell me what to say."

"You know he's a thief, right?" Clint asked. "That for years he's been stealing from the dead."

Ivan looked nervous.

"I don't know nothin' like that, Mr. Adams," he said. "I just do my job."

"He doesn't tell you to take valuables from the cadavers?" Clint asked.

"No, sir," Ivan said. "I only work on the coffins."

They turned and started to walk back.

"Were you there when he put Mrs. Lake's husband in his coffin?" Clint asked.

"I—I guess so."

"You only guess so?"

"I help him put most of the bodies in, after I've finished with the coffin."

"And who puts the lid on?"

"He does."

"Have you ever seen him put anything else in a coffin?"

"L-like what?"

"Something valuable."

"No, sir," Ivan said. "I never see stuff like that."

They reached Sally.

"All right, Ivan," Clint said. "You can go in and tell Jagger I finished with you."

"Thank you, sir."

The little man went inside.

"What did he say?" Sally asked.

"Nothing," Clint said. "He's scared stiff."

"Like everybody else."

Clint nodded.

"What now?" she asked.

"Let's wait for him and see what he has to say."

Chapter Eighteen

Ivan went into the backroom, where Jagger and Rance were waiting.

"What did he say?" Jagger asked.

"He asked me questions."

"And?"

"I answered them."

"Did you tell him what he wanted to hear?" Jagger asked.

"No, boss. I told him nothin'."

"You answered his questions but told him nothin'."

"Yes."

Jagger smiled.

"Good man."

"You want me to take him now, boss?" Rance asked, hoping the answer would be "no."

"Don't be a fool," Jagger said. "He'd kill you before you could draw your gun."

"I can take him from behind."

"Not yet," Jagger said. "I'm still making up my mind how to handle him. The woman might be the way to go."

"How's that?" Rance asked "Kill her?"

"Don't be stupid," Jagger said. "If I can buy her off, she'll call him off and there won't be any trouble."

"So what are ya gonna do now?" Rance asked.

"I'll go out and talk to them," Jagger said. "You two stay here."

"Yes, boss," Ivan said.

"Rance, help Ivan with those coffins," Jagger said, indicating a stack of caskets against the wall.

"To do what with 'em?" Rance asked.

"Whatever Ivan tells you to do," Jagger said. "I'll be right back."

Jagger left the backroom, saw that Clint and the woman were standing outside, and went to join them.

***

Clint saw Jagger step out and waited.

"Did you get what you wanted?" the undertaker asked.

"You know I didn't," Clint said. "He told me what you told him to."

"Not at all," Jagger said. "Ivan is his own man."

"Ivan is as afraid of you as the rest of this town."

"That's nonsense," Jagger said. "We're friends. He's been with me a long time."

"Which means you'll lie, and he'll swear to it."

Jagger looked at Sally.

"I'll have your husband's coffin dug up and put on a buckboard," he told her. "You can pick it up any time."

"That won't buy me off, you know," she said.

"I'm just tryin' to do somethin' for you, Mrs. Lake."

"I want my husband's things," she said. "There was a watch, a money clip, a stick pin—"

"I'm going to have Ivan look for those things," Jagger said. "We'll see what we can do."

Jagger then looked at Clint.

"Can I do anythin' else for you?"

"I'll let you know," Clint said.

He and Sally turned and walked away.

"That's it?" Sally asked him in a low tone.

"Not at all," Clint said, "but let's allow him to dig your husband up before we do anything else."

"And in the meantime?"

"I have another idea," Clint said. "You said the doctor told you your husband died during the night, of a heart attack?"

"Yes."

"Let's go and talk to him. Maybe he knows something."

"The doctor's not a him," she said.

"A female doctor? In this town?"

"I think you're going to like her," Sally said.

***

Sally led Clint to the doctor's office, which was just off the main street in an alley. There was a shingle hanging on a post that said: DOCTOR E. SAUNDERS.

"What's the E. for?" Clint asked.

"I don't know," Sally said. "I never asked."

Clint tried the door, found it unlocked and opened it. They stepped inside, into a waiting room with a sofa and a couple of chairs.

"She has an office in there," Sally said, pointing to another door. "And an examining room further back. She also has a few beds for patients who can't leave."

"So it's a hospital."

"Not quite," Sally said.

Clint stepped to the door and knocked.

"I'm with a patient," a woman's voice called. "Just have a seat and wait."

"Let's sit," Clint said. They shared the sofa.

"What's she like?"

"In her forties," Sally said, "A very striking woman. And she seems competent. I was in a panic, and she handled me quite well. She calmed me down and then talked to me about my husband."

"You said she gave you something?"

"A sedative," Sally said. "It knocked me right out. When I woke up, my husband was in the ground."

"Where did you wake up?"

"Here, in one of her beds."

"Did she tell you why he was buried so quickly."

"She said I'd have to talk to the undertaker about that?"

Clint was going to ask another question, but the door opened and a woman in a white coat stepped out, leading another, older woman.

Chapter Nineteen

Doctor Saunders led the woman to the front door and said, "Now Emily, take those pills I gave you and I'll see you in two weeks."

"Thank you, Doctor," the woman said, and left.

The doctor closed the door and turned to face Clint and Sally, who stood up. Clint saw that Sally was right. The doctor was very striking, with strong features and very clear, smooth skin. She was tall, about five-nine, and filled out her white coat very nicely.

"What can I do for you?" she asked. "Which one is sick?"

"Doctor," Clint said, "do you remember Mrs. Lake?"

Sally took off the hat she had been wearing since they hit the trail.

"Of course," Doctor Saunders said. "Your husband—how are you?"

"I've been better," Sally said.

The doctor looked at Clint.

"And you are her . . . lawyer?"

"No," Clint said, "my name is Clint Adams. We're here in Hays to recover Mrs. Lake's husband, and his belongings."

"How can I help with this?"

"Could we go into your office and talk?" Clint asked.

"Certainly. This way."

Clint and Sally followed her through the other door. It was a well-appointed office with a large, oak desk and a couple of visitor's wooden chairs.

"Have a seat," Doctor Saunders said, sitting behind her desk. "I have another patient in fifteen minutes. You have til then."

They sat across the desk from her.

"I'm here to recover Mrs. Lake's property from the undertaker," Clint explained.

"Property she accused him of stealing," Saunders said, "I remember."

"You're aware that he steals from the dead, aren't you?" Clint asked.

"I'm aware of no such thing," she replied.

"All right," Clint said, "let's put that aside for the moment. What did Mr. Lake die of?"

"I figured it was a heart attack. There wasn't a mark on him. Besides, he died lying in bed beside his wife. Why, what are you thinking?" the doctor asked. "That somebody killed him. Surely, Mrs. Lake would have noticed."

"That's true enough," Clint said.

Doctor Saunders looked pointedly at Sally. Clint knew what she was thinking. What if his wife killed him? That still didn't explain why there wasn't a mark on him.

"Tell me, Doctor," Clint said. "All this I'm hearing about Jagger causing the death of people who cross him. Have you examined those people?"

"Of course, I have."

"And I understand they never have a mark on them."

"That's right," she said. "It's very strange, but not unheard of."

"Are you calling their deaths heart attack related, as well?"

"I don't see what else," she said. "People have been known to drop dead from unknown causes."

"And Jagger can take credit for all of them."

"People give him credit," she corrected. "He never steps up and takes it."

"But he doesn't deny it, either, does he?"

"He never says a word."

"When you saw Mr. Lake, what condition was the body in?" Clint asked.

"He was lying in bed, wearing a nightshirt."

"Did you see his clothes? Examine them?"

"No, why would I?"

"I just wanted to know if you saw his personal effects."

"No."

"What happened after you gave Mrs. Lake that sedative?"

"She slept a few hours in one of my beds."

"And during that time, Jagger came in and collected the body?"

"Yes."

"And his clothing and belongings."

"I assume so."

"So you never saw them."

"I don't believe so."

"Doctor, are you friends with Jagger?"

"No, we simply work together when the need arises."

"Are you afraid of him?"

"I think we're done here, Mr. Adams," she said. "I have to get ready for my next patient." She stood up. "I'll walk you out."

She led Clint and Sally from the room to the front door.

"If there's anything else I can do for you, let me know," she said.

"I might have some more questions."

"I meant if you have need of my medical services," the doctor said, "which I suspect you will, at some point. Good day."

She closed the door, firmly.

***

As Clint and Sally walked away from the doctor's office, Sally said, "She wasn't much help."

"No," Clint said, "but you were right about one thing."

"What's that?"

"She's striking."

"I'm so glad you liked her," Sally said, sarcastically. "What's next?"

"I'm going to stay on both Jagger and Ivan," Clint said. "One of them might break."

"Or Jagger may try to kill you."

"I don't think he'd be able to do it without leaving a mark on me, do you?"

Chapter Twenty

Clint told Sally to go to her room, freshen up and he would come by later to take her to dinner.

"What are you going to do?"

"I'm going to let Jagger and Ivan see me watching them."

"Hoping to make them nervous?"

"Hoping to make them wonder what I'm going to do next," Clint said. "I also might go and talk to the sheriff."

"I thought you said he wasn't very helpful."

"I'm willing to give him another chance."

As Sally walked away from him, Clint wondered if he should have taken the Colt New Line back from her?

***

Clint made his first stop the sheriff's office, hoping to find the man there. He found the door unlocked, but the sheriff wasn't inside. He was wondering what to do next when the man came from across the street.

"Mr. Adams," Barkley said. "I'm just comin' back from doin' my rounds. Come on in. I've got some coffee on the stove. It'll be a little strong by now."

"The stronger the better," Clint said, following him into the office.

Barkley hung his hat on a hook, then went right to the stove to pour two cups of coffee. Clint found some comfort from the fact that the lawman kept his gun on in the office. It meant he showed some sign of being a real lawman.

"There ya go," the sheriff said, handing Clint a cup, and then sitting behind his desk. "What's on your mind?"

"I think you know."

"That again? Are you having any luck?"

Clint sat.

"I met and talked with Jagger."

"Ahh, and?"

"I don't like him."

"Nobody likes the undertaker, as a rule," Barkley said. "Did you find out anything?"

"Well, he's willing to give Mrs. Lake her husband's body."

"There wasn't much else he could say about that."

"He's having it dug up and is giving her the coffin and a buckboard to transport it."

"Hmm, 'giving' is an odd word for something Jagger's doing."

"I was thinking that, too, but he might be trying to get on her good side."

"That'd be smart," Barkley said, "but it's odd. Jagger usually does things for his own benefit."

"Getting on her good side might be to his benefit, but it's not going to happen. He'll never convince her he doesn't know where her husband's watch is, among other things."

"Well, you prove to me he took her husband's things and I'll lock 'im up."

"I'd like to believe that Sheriff," Clint said. "What can you tell me about Ivan?"

"You think Ivan took the things?"

"It's possible, isn't it?"

"I don't think so," Barkley said. "He's been with Jagger a long time. He does whatever the undertaker asks him to do."

"Just out of curiosity, how many other men does Jagger have?" Clint asked.

"I'm not really sure," Barkley said. "He's got a few gravediggers, some ranch hands, people runnin' other businesses he owns."

"How many guns?"

"I'm not sure, but there are guns in town he could press into service for the right price. I still think your best bet is to convince the woman to go back to Kansas City with her husband's body and be satisfied."

"At this point, even if that satisfied her, it wouldn't satisfy me."

"Why get involved at all?"

"That was a question to ask me a few days ago," Clint said. "But now, I can't see walking away from an undertaker who steals from the dead. I can't just turn the other way."

"That's too bad," Barkley said. "This is gonna get messy."

"Yes," Clint said, "it probably is."

"You're not gonna be able to do things the way you usually do, Adams. Jagger never carries a gun."

"Sheriff," Clint said, "you have no idea how I usually conduct myself."

"With that Clint turned and left the office.

***

Sheriff Barkley sat there a few moments, going over the conversation in his head and sipping his coffee. The best thing for him to do was probably go and have a talk with Jagger. But he was starting to think that the

Gunsmith might be the best thing to happen to this town in years. If he managed to get rid of Jagger, that would be a big foot off the necks of most people in town.

Barkley had been sheriff too long to overly turn against the undertaker. He managed to do his job the way he saw fit, except when it came to Jagger. It certainly wouldn't be a problem for him if the undertaker suddenly disappeared. He had often thought of making that happen, himself, but he wasn't a killer. Certainly not while wearing a badge.

So, the best course of action the lawman figured to take was to just wait for Clint Adams to resolve the problem however he decided.

Chapter Twenty-One

From the sheriff's office, Clint went to the undertakers. He tried to get a look inside without being seen. He managed to determine that Jagger and Ivan were still there. Then he took up position across the way. He stood outside a saloon called The White Lance. He watched for an hour, never seeing either man in the doorway. After that he went into the saloon, got a beer and did something he almost never did—he took a table by the window so he could continue to watch. After several hours he hadn't seen anyone go in or out. Of course, they could have been using a back door.

He considered going around back to have a look, but it was getting on toward dinner time and he told Sally he would meet her at her hotel room. So he left the saloon and started walking toward the hotel.

***

Jagger had an office off to one side of the shop. Ivan knocked on the door and entered.

"Adams is gone," the little man said. "He's no longer watchin' us."

"Very good." Jagger stood. "I'll return to the ranch now. Where's Rance?"

"In the back room," Ivan said. "He seemed entranced by the cadavers."

"Tell him to get the buggy ready and bring it around back."

"Yes, sir."

It had been a profitable day for an undertaker, but for Jagger not so much. None of the cadavers that came in that day had any valuables worth taking. And if they did, he might not have been able to take them with Clint Adams watching. He was going to have to figure a way to get rid of Clint Adams and the woman without attracting too much attention. The last thing he needed was a federal marshal poking a nose into Hays.

If Adams died, it was going to have to be of natural causes . . .

***

Clint knocked on her door and when she answered he saw she had changed from trail clothes to a dress.

"You look very pretty," he said. "I didn't have time to wash up, myself."

"You're fine," she said. "You can just wash your hands in my basin."

"Thanks, I'll do that."

He entered the room, and she closed the door. She sat on the bed while he poured some water into the basin and washed. He would have liked to clean up a little more but decided to keep his shirt on.

She watched him with what he could only describe as "hungry eyes," but they didn't have time for that.

"All right, let's go. You must be hungry," he said.

"Oh yes," she said, "I am."

He opened the door and held it, making it clear what he meant. She took a deep breath, sighed and went out the door.

"I thought we'd eat in the hotel," he said. "It's easier."

"I have no problem with that."

They went down to the lobby and were shown to a table in the back. They passed among the other diners with not one glance, which suited Clint. When they sat, they both ordered a steak dinner, figuring it was something safe. A steak, cooked almost any way, was edible.

"Did you accomplish anything while I was wasting time in my room?" she asked.

He told her about his conversation with the sheriff, and then described his time watching the undertaker's shop.

"So, in other words, nothing," she commented.

"Well, the sheriff claims he'll jail Jagger if I can prove he's a thief."

"Did you believe him?"

"I believe he meant it when he said it," Clint said. "Whether he'll do it or not remains to be seen."

"Do you think he's working with the undertaker?"

"Not really," Clint said. "I believe he's not working against Jagger, but I don't think he's in the undertaker's employ."

"Why do you believe that?"

"He's had his badge for a long time," Clint said. "Except for Jagger, I think the sheriff wants to do his job right."

"Then he won't care if you kill Jagger."

"I think you're right about that," Clint said, "but I want to accomplish our goals without killing."

"Maybe I needed a different gunfighter on my side," she said.

"I'm not a gunfighter, Sally," he said. "And if that's what you want, I can recommend a few."

"No, no," she said. "I'm sorry. I'm just frustrated, I didn't mean to insult you. Tell me what your next move is going to be."

"I think I'll talk to the doctor again."

"About what?"

"The people who died of a heart attack, or natural causes," Clint said. "I'd like to look into that a little more."

"Do you want me to come with you?" Sally asked. "I think she had her eye on you."

"That's silly," Clint said. "She's a professional."

"You men," she said, "sometimes you're so dense. She's a woman, and sometimes it takes another woman to see what's right in front of your face."

The waiter came with their plates, and they waited while he served them.

"All right," she said, "so go see the doctor on your own, but don't be surprised if she ends of examining you."

Chapter Twenty-Two

Reluctantly, after dinner Sally went back to her room.

"Don't forget," she said, before Clint left. "I warned you."

"I still think you're wrong," he told her.

He left the hotel and walked to the doctor's office. He knocked on the door several times, but apparently the doctor was not there. He was about to leave when he heard a window open over his head. He looked up and saw Doctor Saunders' face.

"Hello!" she called. "Do you need help?"

"Doctor, it's Clint Adams. I'd like to talk to you some more."

"So you're not sick?" she asked.

"No," he said, "I'm feeling fine."

"Well, I'm not in my office, but come around the back and up the stairs."

"Thank you."

He went to the back of the building and up a rickety stairway. When he got to the top he knocked.

"Come in," she said, opening the door.

He entered and she closed the door behind them. He looked around and was surprised to see well-furnished living quarters.

"Yeah, I live over my office, so even when I'm not there my patients can get to me."

She was not dressed in a professional manner. Instead of a skirt she was wearing jeans, and a plaid shirt. He had to admit she looked very fetching.

"Can I get you something?" she asked. "I just finished dinner and was going to have some coffee."

"That sounds good."

"I'll be right along. Have a seat."

As she left the room, he noticed a clean scent in the air. It was nothing perfumed, like was found in most woman's homes. As he told Sally, the woman was professional, even her home was spotless.

When she came back into the room with a tray, it held a pot of coffee, two cups and two slices of pie.

"I had an apple pie leftover from yesterday."

"That works."

She poured a cup of coffee, handed it to him, then followed with a nice hunk of pie, and a fork. She had a smaller helping of everything.

"This is very good. Did you bake it?" he asked, tasting the pie.

"I didn't," she said. "One of my patients gave it to me as a fee. But I made the coffee."

"It's very good." He put the pie and coffee down on the table in front of them.

"Now, what can I do for you, Mr. Adams?"

"I wanted to talk a little more about those people who also died without a mark on them."

"Ah, I thought that's what this would be about."

"Are you sure there was nothing definite in their manner of death?" he asked. "Poison, maybe."

"There was nothing to indicate they were poisoned," she said. "There's usually some residue left behind, some odor or even color. In these cases, there was nothing."

"How many of them had a connection to Jagger? Maybe they were in business with him?"

"Each of the dead did have a business in town," she said, "but none of them were in business with him. However, each of them was seen in a heated conversation with him the day before they died."

"And that wasn't enough to make the sheriff act?" Clint asked.

"The sheriff talked to a lot of people after each death, including the undertaker."

"And found nothing suspicious?"

"Apparently not," she said. "Nothing he could act on, anyway."

"And if he did have something to act on, do you think he would?" Clint asked.

"You know," she said, "I've been the doctor here for some time, and I've watched the sheriff change."

"In what way?"

"He used to be very serious about his job," she said, "but when these deaths started to occur—well, he started to give Jagger a rather wide berth. It's as if he's a different man when it comes to dealing with the undertaker."

"So, you're saying when it comes to Jagger, he looks the other way."

"I suppose so," she said. "Or maybe I don't know what I'm saying, at all. More coffee?"

"No, thank you." Clint had finished his coffee and pie while they were talking.

"Let me clear these things away," she said. starting to get up.

"That's okay," Clint said, "I should be going."

"No, please," she said. "Just wait until I clean up."

"Well, all right," he said, sitting back down.

She gathered up the plates and cups and carried them all back to the kitchen with the coffee pot. When she came back through the door, he couldn't help but notice that a couple of buttons on her shirt had come undone.

"Whew," she said, sitting back down, "it's hot in the kitchen."

"I should be going, Doctor," he said, "unless there's something else on your mind?"

"Well," she said, touching his knee, "now that you mention it, —are you and Mrs. Lake . . . involved?"

"Oh, no," he said. "I'm just trying to help out. No one else seemed able to do anything."

"And you thought you could?"

"I don't need evidence to act, as Sheriff Barkley does, and I don't have a jurisdictional problem, as Sheriff Wilson in Kansas City does."

"So you're a man who has his own rules?"

"I guess you could say that."

"Interesting," she said, putting the flat of her hand on his thigh and rubbing it. He could feel the heat through the fabric of his jeans. It made him remember the warning he had gotten from Sally Lake.

Chapter Twenty-Three

"Doctor—"

"Please," she said, squeezing his thigh, "call me Evelyn, Clint."

"Evelyn," he said, "I only came up here to talk—"

"I know why you came up here," she said, "but I also know why I asked you up here."

"Evelyn—"

"I'm a woman with needs, Clint," she said, "and I can't satisfy them in this town. I must retain the respect of these people if I'm to do my job, and it's taken me a long time to establish that. Usually, if I need to satisfy a base desire, I have to leave town and go somewhere else. Even then, I often don't find what I'm looking for. You see, most men treat sex the same way. They're in a hurry to satisfy their own desires, with no thought of the woman. To them, all women are whores who are here as a receptacle. But I know you have a reputation with a gun, and with women."

"Well—"

She didn't allow Clint to get a word in.

"So when I realized who you were, I saw a chance to satisfy myself without having to leave town to find a man I could be with, without destroying my reputation. After all, you'll be leaving town soon, and you already have a woman, so you won't become infatuated."

"Sally Lake is not my woman, Evelyn," Clint said. "I'm essentially working for her."

"That's even better," she said. "If you can help her get what she wants without becoming emotionally involved, you can do the same for me."

"Evelyn, I don't think—"

"Please," she said, standing, "give me a chance to present myself properly."

With the top two buttons of her shirt already undone, she unbuttoned it the rest of the way, and took it off. Her full breasts were barely encased in an undergarment, which she also peeled off. Her breasts were large, almost pear-shaped, and for a woman who was probably in her mid-forties, she was still very firm. Her nipples were a dusky color, and very large.

"What do you think?" she asked. "If you don't find me attractive, I'll stop here."

Clint wet his lips and said, "Uh, no, don't stop."

Evelyn Saunders smiled and said, "Excellent."

She sat on the sofa to remove her boots, then stood again to discard her trousers, leaving herself totally nude. She was a statuesque woman who took his breath away.

She came close, bathing him in her heat, and pulled him to his feet. Pressing her naked body to him, she kissed him, a kiss that went on for some time. Eventually, she moaned into his mouth and broke the kiss.

"First, what do we do with this gun?" she asked.

"I just need it to be within reach," he told her.

"Even at a time like this?"

"I can't ever afford to be without it."

"Come with me, then," she said. She turned and walked away. "He watched her for a few seconds. She had a fine, firm ass and long, sleek legs. He followed and she led him to a bedroom.

"Where do you want to put the gun?" she asked.

"I'll hang it on the bedpost."

"Well, go ahead, and then get your clothes off. It's been a while for me, and I'm getting impatient."

While he hung the gunbelt on the bedpost and undressed, she pulled down the bed spread, revealing floral patterned sheets. When he was naked, he turned and found her on the bed, watching him. Her eyes took him in hungrily.

"Oh my," she said, staring at his already hard cock. "Bring that over here."

"If I do this for you, I'm going to need something from you."

"You think this will just be for me?" she asked. "Don't worry. You'll enjoy it."

"I know I will," he said. "But I can do it like all those other men you talked about, or I can make sure you enjoy it. It's your choice."

"What is it you want? Money?"

"No, not money," Clint said. "Just some information."

"If I have it, it's yours."

"All right, then."

He got into bed with her, and she reached for him anxiously. As she closed her hand around his penis, he realized that Sally's warning had been right. Not that he minded, much.

***

Jagger finished his dinner at home, then left the table and went to the office he kept in his house. He had just seated himself at his desk when there was a knock at the door and the cook answered it. Rance Newman came walking in. Jagger had told him to come to the house after he had his dinner in the mess hall.

"Sit down, Rance," Jagger said.

The man seated himself and waited.

"I need to deal with Clint Adams," the undertaker said.

"You want him dead?" Rance asked.

"I'd prefer he leave town and not come back," Jagger said. "You get my drift?"

"You want him dead, but you don't want Hays to be known as the town where the Gunsmith was killed."

"That's right," Jagger said. "I don't want people comin' here the way they flocked to Deadwood to see where Hickok died."

"So, you want me to get 'im out of town and do him on the trail," Rance said.

"That's right," Jagger said. "Figure out how to do it, but not until I say so. I still want to see if I can deal with him my way. Figure out how many men it'll take you."

"That's gonna be expensive," Rance said.

"Remember, I hired you to be my foreman," Jagger reminded him.

"There ain't much to be foreman of, around here," Rance pointed out. "You don't run no cattle, or horses. So this'll be a different job. It'll cost more."

Jagger leaned back in his chair and said, "It'll be worth it."

Chapter Twenty-Four

Clint gave Evelyn Saunders as much pleasure as she could take, and more. He covered her body with kisses before nestling his face down between her legs. He worked her with his lips and tongue until she was soaking the bed with her juices. Finally, as she began to tremble, but before she could scream, he mounted her and drove himself into her. Mindful of her past experiences with men, he began to move in-and-out of her slowly.

"Oh God," she breathed, as she moved in rhythm with him. "Oh Jesus, you're killing me."

"You want me to stop?"

"Hell, no!"

And he didn't stop until a tidal wave of pleasure washed over her, leaving her limp and out of breath.

He rolled and lay side-by-side with her, catching his own breath.

"Mrs. Lake must be waiting for you," she said.

"I've got plenty of time," he said. "Remember what I told you about information?"

"I do."

"I could leave now, or I could stay, and we can have more of the same," he said. "But first I need you to keep your end of the bargain."

She rubbed her face vigorously with both hands, then said, "What do you want to know?"

"How did Jagger kill those people without leaving a mark on them?" he asked.

She turned in bed to face him and said, "I can't tell you that."

"Because you're afraid of him?"

"Because I don't know," she said. "I don't know if it was Jagger, and if it was, I don't know how. I couldn't find a cause of death on any of them."

"And that's the truth?" he asked.

"Yes, it's the truth."

"Then tell me how he could've done it."

"He could have poisoned them, but most poisons leave a trace—a color, an odor, something. I didn't see anything."

"Did you look? Did you really look?"

She laid down on her back and stared at the ceiling.

"No, not really," she said. "I did what any doctor would do, but I can't say I went further."

"Evelyn, are you afraid of him?"

She bit her lips, then said, "Yes."

"If I brought you a body, could you look deeper for something?"

"I—I suppose so."

"If you found something you could give it to the sheriff. Then we'd see what the sheriff would really do"

"A-all right, but where are you going to get a body?"

"You leave that up to me," he said.

"A-all right."

"Now," he said, putting a hand on her hip, "do you want to go again?"

She caught her breath and said, "God help me, it makes me sound like a horrible person, but yes, I do."

"Well, if you're horrible," he said, turning to her, "then so am I."

***

While they were being horrible people together, several times, Sally Lake sat in her room, thinking about Clint and the doctor being together. She had no claim on Clint Adams, but she felt jealousy. She had warned Clint about Doc Saunders' intentions, but after all, Clint was a man and a woman like Evelyn Saunders would be hard to resist.

She walked to the window and looked out; the darkened street was empty. If the undertaker kept his word, she would be getting her husband's body back, to bury in Kansas City. Maybe she should be satisfied with that and tell Clint he didn't owe her anything. But it seemed as if Clint was bound and determined to stop the undertaker from stealing from any more bodies. She wished Clint would just end it, and they could go home.

***

The final time they coupled, it was with Evelyn on top, and she bounced around on him like a wild animal. She pressed her hands down flat on his chest and rode him for all she was worth. Finally, she finished with a muffled scream, just seconds before Clint exploded inside of her . . .

***

When they were done, she watched from the bed as he got dressed and strapped on his gun. The last thing he did was sit on the bed to pull on his boots.

He looked at her before standing and put his hand on her bare thigh.

"So was that terrible?" he asked.

"As long as the both of us were terrible," she said, with a smile, "it was just fine."

Evelyn got up and pulled on a robe so she could walk him to the door.

"When will you have a body for me?" she asked.

"Probably tomorrow," he said.

"That quickly?"

"Jagger promised Sally her husband's body," he said. "Where should we bring it once we have it?"

"Around back," she said. "I'll let you in."

"Good," Clint said. "It will depend on when Jagger gives up the body."

"But" she said, "he could be lying."

"Yes, he could be," Clint said. "We're going to find out."

Chapter Twenty-Five

Clint returned to his hotel and went directly to his room. He decided to avoid Sally's I-told-you-so until breakfast. He was surprised when, over bacon-and-eggs, she didn't say anything like that.

All she said, was, "How did it go last night?"

"Fine," he said. "Doc Saunders says if we bring her your husband's body, she'll do a full examination to see if she can determine what actually killed him."

"But why would the undertaker kill Charles, they never met."

"Are you sure?" Clint asked. "Did your husband ever go out while you were in town?"

"We were only in town one day . . . but yes, he did go out for a while, while I stayed in the room."

"To do what?"

"He didn't say."

"Didn't you ask him?"

"One of the reasons we stayed married so long was that I never asked Charles about his business."

"Wasn't he a storekeeper?"

"Well, yes, but I always felt he had some kind of secret business, where most of his money came from."

"Illegal business?"

"I don't know, but why else would it be a secret?"

"So was he using his legitimate business to hide the proceeds from his illegal business?"

"It could be," she said. "I just always preferred not to know."

"Well, maybe whatever his illegal business was got him killed," Clint said. "If we go ahead with this, you're going to find out what it was."

"I suppose that's true," she said, glumly.

"Sally," Clint asked, "how much money did your husband leave you?"

"I don't know," she said. "I haven't seen his lawyer, yet."

"Is his lawyer in Kansas City?"

"Yes."

"Well, you can see him when you go back."

"Would you come with me?" she asked.

"There's really no need—"

"I'd just feel a lot better."

"All right," Clint said, "I can do that. But we have a few things to clean up here, first."

"So you're thinking the undertaker didn't only steal from my husband, but killed him as well?"

"It's possible."

"And if we prove that, you think the sheriff will arrest him?" she asked.

"I think he just might," Clint replied. "But first we have to get the body to the doctor."

"When do we do that?"

"It will depend on when Jagger unearths the body and puts in on a buckboard for you. The only thing is, we can't let him know that's what we're doing."

"How do you propose we do that?"

"We could let Jagger know that we've given up trying to nail him, and we're leaving town. Then we take the body around to the back of her office."

"Do you think he'd believe that?"

"It'll depend on how we present it."

"I'm sure you have an idea how to do that."

"I have several," he said, and proceeded to outline them while they ate breakfast . . .

***

While he ate his breakfast, the undertaker sent for Rance Newman. The foreman arrived as he was finishing up. Jagger let the man stand there and didn't offer him anything.

"I've got a job for you," he said.

"A job other than dealing with the Gunsmith?"

"Yes," Jagger said, "and you'll do this one first. I need you to take a couple of men to Boot Hill, dig up Charles Lake's body and put it, coffin and all, onto a buckboard. Then drive it to town to my shop and leave the rig there."

"Is that all?"

"Yes, that's all. But don't forget you have to bring me your ideas for dealing with Adams."

"Yes, sir. Should I go now?"

"Yes," Jagger said, "go."

Rance left the house. He wasn't happy with the way Jagger treated him, but he was satisfied with his pay. And for dealing with the Gunsmith his pay would be a lot more.

***

When Clint finished explaining his ideas Sally said, "Okay, whichever way you want to go, I'm with you."

"All right, let's see if Jagger dug up your husband."

Clint paid the bill and then they left the hotel and walked to the undertaker's place. Jagger wasn't there, but Ivan was. He left Sally outside and went in.

"Jagger said he'd dig up Mrs. Lake's husband."

"He told me," Ivan said. "He has three men up at Boot Hill now. They'll bring it here."

"Okay," Clint said. "When it gets here, I want to open it."

"The coffin? You wanna look inside?"

"That's right."

"You think he's not in there?"

"I think he might be in there with a few other things," Clint said.

"Like what?"

"That's what I'm going to find out. When will they be here with the coffin?"

"An hour."

"Good. I'll be back and Mrs. Lake will be with me. You'll open the coffin for us."

"Yeah, okay."

Clint left and joined Sally outside.

"Everything okay?" she asked.

"We're set," Clint told her. "Back here in one hour."

"What do we do until then?"

"Let's get a drink. There's a saloon down the street."

"What about my room?" she asked, touching his arm.

"Come on, Sally, we've only got an hour. If I get lost in your arms, we'll never get back here. Let's just get that drink."

Chapter Twenty-Six

Rance and two other men dug up Charles Lake's coffin and loaded it onto a buckboard.

"That's harder than plantin' 'em," one man said, wiping his face and neck with a neckerchief.

"What now?" the other man asked.

"We take the box over to the undertaker's."

"Ain't we doin' this the other way around?" the man with the kerchief asked.

"Look, the boss knows what he's doin'," Rance said. "We just take the whole rig over there and drop it in back. Then we're done."

"Good," the other man said, "I don't wanna carry this thing no more."

All three of them climbed on board and Rance shook the reins at the two horses to get them going.

***

They found a small saloon called The Six Shooter, and it was cleaner than the last one. They had a beer each, nursing them.

"Do you think Jagger will be there?" she asked.

"I doubt it," Clint said.

"What are we going to do after we open the coffin?"

"We'll take a look inside. When we don't find anything, we'll act satisfied. Then we'll take it over to the doc's."

"Ivan'll let us do that?"

"We're not going to tell him what we're doing," Clint said. "For all he knows, we're heading for Kansas City."

"I almost wish we were."

"Are you ready to give up?"

"Oh no," Sally said. "Not after all we've gone through. I want to see this to the end."

"Then let's go."

***

Clint and Sally entered the undertaker's shop, Ivan took them out back to where the buckboard was.

"Pry the top off, Ivan."

"Yes, sir."

Ivan climbed on the back of the buckboard and loosened the top of the coffin.

"That'll do," Clint said.

"Of course."

Ivan stepped down and Clint turned to Sally.

"Can I help you up?" he asked.

"I don't think so, Clint," Sally said. "You do the honors."

Clint climbed on the back of the buckboard and removed the top of the coffin. He leaned it against the side of the box, and then looked inside.

"What's he wearing?" Sally asked.

"A grey suit."

"Yes, that was in his luggage."

"What else am I looking for?" Clint asked.

"A pocket watch, a ring with a black stone, and matching cuff links."

Clint examined the body.

"None of those things are here," Clint said. "Ivan?"

"I—I don't know what happened to them," the little man said.

"Sally, I think you should come up here," Clint said.

"But why?"

"I just want to make sure this body is really Charles Lake."

"Oh, all right."

Clint reached down and helped her onto the buckboard. She kept her eyes averted as long as she could but finally gazed into the box.

"Oh my God!" she said.

"Well?" Clint asked.

She looked at Clint.

"It's not him."

"What?" Ivan said. He climbed up onto the buckboard and looked into the coffin.

"So?" Clint asked.

"That's the man we buried," Ivan said. "Mr. Jagger said he was Charles Lake."

"Are you sure your men didn't dig up the wrong coffin?" Clint asked.

"No, sir," Ivan said, "I mean, yessir, it's him."

Clint looked at Sally.

"It's not him," Sally said. "That's not my husband."

Clint went through the dead man's pocket but found no identification.

"Ivan," Clint said. "We're going to need the sheriff."

"Yessir."

The little man dropped down from the buckboard and hurried away.

***

"Wait a minute, Adams," Sheriff Barkley said. "First you accuse Jagger of stealing the dead man's jewelry, and now you're accusing him of stealin' the dead man?"

"Sheriff, the only thing I know is that Charles Lake's wife says this body is not him."

"Then who is he?" Barkley asked. "And where's the real Charles Lake?"

"I've got another question," Clint said.

"What's that?" the lawman asked.

"Is Charles Lake even dead?"

"Now wait," Sally said. "If Charles isn't dead, where is he? And who's this?"

Chapter Twenty-Seven

"Sally," Clint said, "when you woke up that morning, are you sure Charles was dead?"

"I—well—I thought he was. He seemed dead." She looked at Clint. "The doctor said he was dead."

"That's right, she did," Clint said. He looked at Barkley. "Can we get her over here for an identification?"

"I'll do that right now."

As Barkley left, Clint asked Ivan, "When is Mr. Jagger due in?"

"Not til this afternoon."

"Can you get word to him to come earlier?"

"Yessir."

"Do it."

"Yessir, but—"

"But what?"

"What should I tell him?"

"Nothing about the body," Clint said. "Just tell him he's needed."

"Yessir."

Ivan went off to send for Jagger.

"This is crazy," Sally said. "What do we do now?"

"The doctor will get here before Jagger," Clint said. "We'll deal with that first."

"What if she says my husband is dead?"

"First we have to determine if she ever saw your husband's body," Clint said. "If she identifies the body in the box as your husband, that'll be because Jagger presented it to her as Charles Lake."

"So that way it all comes down to Jagger," she said.

"There's something else to think about."

"What's that?"

"What if Charles was in on it?"

"What? Why would he fake his own death?" she asked.

"That's something you can tell me," Clint said. "Was he happy?"

"Well, the older he got the more he brooded."

"Was the vacation in St. Louis his idea?"

"As a matter of fact, it was."

"And the stopover in Hays?"

"Yes. Oh my God . . . Charles's still alive?"

"Looks like it could be," Clint said.

Ivan came back in.

"I sent word," Ivan said. "He should be here soon."

"Okay," Clint said, "now we need the doctor."

At that moment Sheriff Barkley came in, leading Doc Saunders.

"What's this all about, Clint?" she asked. "The Sheriff wouldn't let me know."

"We've got something to show you," Clint said.

"What's that?"

"Out back."

Clint led the way out back. They all followed.

"Hey, what's this all about?" Evelyn asked.

"We dug this box up from Charles Lake's gravesite. I want you to look inside and tell me who it is."

"You just told me it's Charles Lake."

"Humor me."

He helped her up onto the bed of the buckboard and she looked inside.

"Well?"

She looked down at the four people staring up at her.

"That's him," she said.

"Charles Lake?"

"Yes."

"Jagger told you this was Lake?"

"Yes. Why?"

"It's not him," Sally said. "It's not my husband."

"What?"

Clint helped her down.

"Is this the body you wanted me to examine?"

"It was when I thought it was Charles Lake."

"Well, if he's not Lake, who is he?"

"We don't know that," Clint said. "But I still want to know how he died."

"Well, we'll have to move him to my office." She looked around. "Jagger's not here?"

"Not yet, but he's on the way."

"Then let's get out of here."

"We'll need help moving him into your office," Clint said.

"I'll help," Barkley said. "I wanna know what's goin' on."

"You'll need somebody else," Clint said.

"Ivan'll help, won't you, Ivan."

"Uh, sure, Sheriff."

"Okay, move it over there so the doc can get started," Clint said.

"What are you gonna do?" Barkley asked.

"I'll wait here for Jagger."

"You think you can get him to talk?"

"Who knows? But at least I can keep him busy until the doc examines the body."

"Okay," the sheriff said to Ivan. "Let's go."

They helped Evelyn into the buckboard seat. Barkley sat next to her and picked up the reins. Ivan rode on the back with the coffin.

"Now what?" Sally asked.

"Now we wait."

***

Before long they heard a rig stop out front.

"Just sit tight and keep quiet," Clint said.

"I know, let you do all the talking."

When Jagger came in, he was alone.

"Adams," he said. "Where's Ivan?"

"He's running an errand."

"What kind of errand?"

"Don't worry," Clint said. "It's your kind."

Chapter Twenty-Eight

"What's my kind of errand?" Jagger asked.

"You know," Clint said, "moving a body."

"You got Lake's body?"

"Your boys dug the coffin up from Charles Lake's gravesite. And guess what? The body inside wasn't him."

"What? What are you talkin' about?"

"Mrs. Lake saw the body in the box," Clint said. "It's not her husband."

"It was him when I put him in the box," Jagger said. "Maybe somebody else switched 'em."

"Come on, Jagger," Clint said. "Lake's not dead and you know it."

"Why would I bury someone else and say it was him?" Jagger asked.

"That's what I'd like to know."

"Where is this body?"

"I'm not really sure, at the moment," Clint said. "Sheriff Barkley left here with it."

"And Ivan?"

"Sure," Clint said. "He needed help moving the body."

"To where?"

Clint shrugged.

"He's going to try to find out who the dead guy is. Oh, and how he died."

"You're lyin'," Jagger said. "She's lyin'. That was Lake, all right."

"What does she gain by lying?" Clint asked. "She wants her husband and his belongings."

"We're back to that, again. I'm kind enough to dig up the body for you, and you pull this."

"We're not the ones trying to pull something, Jagger," Clint said. "With this phony body we're going to prove you're crooked."

Jagger smiled.

"Not unless you can get a dead body to talk."

Sally came out of her seat, yelling, "Where's my husband, you bastard."

Jagger remained calm.

"Mrs. Lake, the last time I saw your husband he was in that coffin. If he's not in there now, I can't help you."

"Easy, Sally," Clint said. "We're going to find the answers."

"I'm afraid I have some work to do," Jagger said. "And I'll have to wait here for Ivan to return, so if you please . . ."

"Sure," Clint said. "We have things to do ourselves. Sally, let's go."

"But Clint—"

"We have to go."

He took her arm and guided her out to the front.

"Clint—" she started.

"We have to get over to the doc's and see if she's found out anything," he told her.

Sally took a deep breath and said, "You're right, but she's going to need time to examine it. Can we get a drink first. I need one."

"Sure," Clint said, "we can go back to The Six Shooter."

They started walking.

***

After Clint and Sally left, Jagger went out the back and found Rance.

"What's goin' on?" the man asked.

"That's what I want to know," Jagger said. "Find Ivan."

"Where do I look?"

"I can only think of one place they'd take the body. If it turns out I'm right, this is what I want you to do . . ."

***

After a drink at The Six Shooter, they started to the doctor's office, but detoured to the sheriff's. He might still be at the doctors, but they stopped and checked. When they walked in, he was at his desk and looked up at them.

"You see the doc?" he asked.

"Not yet," Clint said. "You and Ivan get it into her place?"

"We did," Barkley said, "and when I left, she was getting started."

"How about Ivan?" Clint asked.

"What about him?"

"Did he stay around?"

"No, he left right away to get back to Jagger's place."

"He probably wanted to report back," Clint said. "We'll get over to the doc's and keep an eye on her place, in case Jagger shows up."

"If there's a problem from him, let me know. I'm dyin' to have a reason to bring him in."

"That's good to hear, Sheriff," Sally said.

"Believe me, Mrs. Lake," he said. "I want to help you."

"We'll see you later," Clint said.

He and Sally went out.

"He has quite a different attitude than when I was last here," she said. "I think that has something to do with you."

"Well, whatever the reason, it's good to hear. Let's get to the doc's."

***

When they reached the doctor's office, the front door was locked.

"I guess she doesn't want to be disturbed," Clint said. "Let's go around back."

They found an alley that led to the back. The buckboard was still there, with the empty coffin on the bed.

They tried the back door and found it unlocked. Clint led the way in and down a long hallway. The first door they tried was a storeroom. He figured the doors toward the front went to her office and waiting room. The door he finally opened looked as if it led to an examining room.

"This is it," he said, because there was the man's body on a table. The clothing had been removed and he looked like a lump of grey.

"Doc?" he called. "Doctor Saunders?"

When there was no answer, he moved deeper into the room and went around the table. He stopped short when he saw the doctor lying on the floor.

She was obviously dead, with a knife sticking out of her back.

Sally screamed.

Chapter Twenty-Nine

Clint grabbed Sally by the shoulders, moved her away so that the body of the doctor was out of sight.

"Stay there."

Sally nodded, wordlessly.

Clint leaned over the doctor's body to make sure, but she was dead.

"Who would do this?" Sally asked. "Jagger?"

"He didn't know she was helping us."

"Maybe Ivan told him."

"I don't know if he could've done that soon enough for Jagger to set this up."

"But who else would want her dead?"

"That's a good question. Come on, we better go and get the sheriff."

"I could stay here and . . . keep watch."

"No," he said, "I don't want you here alone."

"Good," she said, "I didn't really want to stay, anyway."

They left the same way they came in.

***

"She didn't deserve this," Sheriff Barkley said, looking down at the body.

"No, she didn't," Clint said. Sally was standing in a corner of the room quietly, arms folded.

"You think it was Jagger?"

"Would he mess his hands, this way?" Clint asked.

"Not likely."

"Then he probably had somebody do it before she could take a close look at this other body."

"I could pick him up for this," Barkley said, "but I can't prove anythin'."

"I have an idea."

"What is it?"

"Let's not let Jagger know we found the body," Clint said. "If we don't tell him she's dead, and he gives away that he knows—"

"—then he's givin' himself away," Barkley finished. "I get it."

"Is there somewhere you can put the body for a day or two?" Clint asked.

"I guess I can put it in the icehouse," Barkley said. "We'll just have to get it there without anyone knowin'."

"You got people you can trust to help you?" Clint asked.

"One or two men," Barkley said. "My deputy and one other."

"Okay, that's good."

"What are you gonna do in the meantime?" Barkley said.

"I'm going to press Jagger harder," Clint said.

"You think you can break him?" Barkley asked.

"Probably not," Clint said. "He's a pretty hard man. But maybe I can force him into a bad move."

Barkley looked at the man on the table.

"What do we do with him?"

"Better put him on ice, too, until we can find out who he is," Clint said.

"Okay," Barkley said. "Check back with me in my office in about an hour."

"Will do."

He went to the corner and guided the silent Sally out of the room.

Outside he asked her, "You want to go back to your hotel room?"

"And be alone? Not on your life," she said. "Where you go, I go."

"Okay," he said, "then let's get back to the undertaker's."

***

When Rance came back to the undertaker's he had Ivan with him.

"Ran into him coming back," he said, pushing the little man ahead of him.

"Was I right?" Jagger asked Rance.

"Yes, sir."

"And did you do what I wanted you to do?"

"Oh, yes sir."

Jagger looked at Ivan.

"The sheriff made me help him move the body, sir," the little man said.

"I understand that, Ivan. Did you see what Rance did?"

"No, sir. He made me wait outside."

"Very good. Rance and I are leaving now, going back to the house. If anyone is looking for me, I won't be back in today."

"Yes, sir."

"You're a good man, Ivan," Jagger said. "Just keep doin' your job."

"Yessir."

"Go outside, now."

Ivan scurried into the back room.

"Now what?" Rance asked.

"Crawl into a hole and pull it in behind you," Jagger said. "Stay out of sight, but let your boys know where you are in case I want you."

"I can do that. What about you?"

"Like I said, I'm going home. I've got to have a talk with my guest."

"Right."

Rance started for the door, but Jagger stopped him.

"Go out the back, just in case someone's watchin'."

"Yessir."

Rance went out the back, moving so quickly he frightened Ivan, who was glad to see the man leave.

Jagger poked his head in the back and said, "I'm going."

"Yessir."

Jagger went out the front door.

Chapter Thirty

Clint decided to take Sally back to the hotel.

"I may have to move quickly," he told her.

"All right."

As they walked to the hotel she said, "I feel so guilty," Sally said.

"About what?"

"If I hadn't insisted on stopping for a drink, maybe you could have saved her."

"Don't feel any guilt," Clint said. "It's not your fault. None of it."

"If it wasn't for me, you wouldn't be here," she said. "I was just so mad and so stubborn."

"It's understandable," Clint said. "And you were probably still in shock."

When they got to the hotel, he walked her to her room, but didn't go in.

"You still have that gun I gave you?" he asked.

"Yes," she said.

"All right," he said. "If anybody but me comes through this door, use it."

"Even the sheriff?"

"Even the sheriff," Clint said. "I'm still not sure about him."

"A-all right," she said, "but please be careful, Clint."

"I will. Now go inside and lock this door."

He waited until he heard the lock, then left.

***

When Clint got back to the shop, Ivan was just coming out of the back room. The little man stopped short and stared.

"Ivan, where's Jagger?"

"Uh, he went home."

"Will he be back?"

"Not today."

"Good. Now you better stay in that back room until I say so. I want to have a look around, and you want to be able to say you didn't see a thing."

"Yes, sir!"

He disappeared.

Clint searched every nook and cranny of the front area and didn't find a thing. He went into the back room, found Ivan working on a coffin with a sander.

"Okay," Clint said, "let's trade places, you in front and me back here."

"Yessir."

Ivan hurried through the door into the front.

Clint did a thorough search of the back area, coffins and all, but didn't find a thing. When he came back out, Ivan was sitting in a chair, waiting.

"Ivan?"

"Yes!" he chirped, standing.

"Is there any place I haven't looked?"

Ivan hesitated, then said, "Well . . ."

"Yes?"

"Mr. Jagger has an office.

"Where?"

"There's a door behind that curtain."

Clint went to the wall, moved the curtain and found the door.

"Ivan . . ."

"Yes, I know," Ivan said. "I'll go in the back."

"Good man."

Ivan went into the back, and Clint opened the door to Jagger's office.

It was a small area, with hardly enough room for the desk and chair. Clint went around the desk, sat in the chair and started going through drawers. There wasn't much there besides papers. When he slammed a bottom drawer shut, he noticed something odd. The drawer looked deeper on the outside than on the inside.

He opened the drawer again, pressed his hand against the bottom, and felt it give then bounce up, as if on a spring. He took papers out of the drawer, then swung the bottom open, revealing a compartment inside.

It was filled with jewelry.

***

Ivan huddled in the back, shivering. He was afraid of Clint Adams, but he was more afraid of Charles Jagger. But he knew he was going to have to do something when Adams left, whether he was afraid or not.

***

Clint stared at the jewelry. He had no doubt that all of it had been stolen from the dead.

He took a few pieces from the compartment. Earrings, broaches, rings—both men and women's—and men's cufflinks and stick pins. He even found a few watches but had no way of knowing if any of this stuff belonged to Charles Lake. He was going to have to bring Sally back here, since Jagger was not returning this evening.

He put all the jewelry back, closed the compartment—making sure it locked into place—then returned the papers and closed the drawer.

He left the small office, making sure the door closed, and pulled the curtain back into place. That done, he went into the backroom.

"Ivan, I'm leaving."

"Did you, uh, find anything, sir?"

"Nothing I could identify," Clint said. "Remember, you're better off if you didn't' see me."

"Yessir."

Chapter Thirty-One

Clint went back to the hotel to collect Sally.

When he knocked on the door, she called out, "Who is it?"

"It's me."

She opened it, with the gun in her hand.

"Stick that back in your belt."

She did.

"Why are you back so soon?" she asked.

"Let's go inside."

They stepped in and closed the door.

"What's wrong, Clint?"

He told her about the secret compartment he found full of jewelry.

"Of course, I couldn't identify any of it, so you better come back with me."

"You didn't bring any of it with you?"

"No, I didn't want Jagger claiming I stole anything. Ivan was there, and although I told him not to say anything, I'm not sure he'll keep quiet. But let's get over there and we'll see if you can pick something out."

"All right."

She got up to grab her jacket.

"And keep that gun in your belt, just in case."

"Right."

They left the hotel.

***

When they reached the undertaker's shop the front door was open, but no one was there.

"Ivan! Ivan!" Clint called.

There was no answer, and the little man was nowhere to be found.

"Come on," he said to Sally, and led her to the little office. When he opened the drawer, he sprang the bottom of it open.

It was empty.

"Where is it?" Sally asked.

"Damn it, Ivan must have taken it all."

"But why?"

"Because he's more afraid of Jagger than he is of me."

"You think he's taking it all to Jagger?"

"I can't figure anything else."

"So what do we do?"

"He's got a head start on us," Clint said, "but we can ride out there."

"To do what?" she asked. "If he gives the jewelry to Jagger, he'll hide it."

"Then we'll do a search of the whole house, if we have to."

"Do you think Mrs. Jagger would let us?"

"No," Clint said, "But we'd better stop and see the sheriff, first. I want him to know we're going there, just in case."

***

"I'm not sure this is the right thing for you to do," the sheriff said.

"Sheriff, all that jewelry must be stolen."

"You can say that, but you can't prove it."

"I'm going to try," Clint said. "All Sally has to do is identify a piece as her husband's."

"If she does that, then I'll move on him," Barkley said. "But if you attack the man in his own home, you'll be in the wrong."

"I'll take that chance. Do you want to come with me?"

"Yes, but I can't."

"Fine, then stay here and wait to hear from me."

Clint and Sally headed for the door.

"One more thing," the lawman said.

"What's that?"

"I can't keep the doctor's death quiet much longer," he said. "I'll have to let the news out tomorrow."

"Why?" Sally asked.

"Some of her patients are looking for her," Barkley said. "Some of them are pretty bad off. I've got to let these people know they need a new doctor. They can go to Sunnyville and see the one there."

"All right," Clint said, "you do what you have to do, and we'll do what we have to do."

***

When Clint and Sally left the sheriff's office, they went to the livery. Clint tried to rent a buggy for Sally, but she refused.

"I told you I used a gun when I was young and on my own," she said. "I also rode horses."

"All right, then."

Clint rented her a 6-year-old bay mare, and saddled his Tobiano. They walked the horses outside, mounted up and headed out.

***

After Clint left the undertaker's shop, Ivan rushed into the office with a leather sack. He opened the drawer, popped the secret compartment, and filled the sack with the jewelry. Then he made sure he closed the compartment and the drawer.

He rushed out back where they kept the team that pulled the funeral carriage, saddled one of the horses, and rode hell-bent-for-leather for Jagger's ranch.

When he got there, he rushed to the door and pounded on it. Martha opened it.

"I have to see the boss!" he blurted.

She stepped aside and allowed him to enter.

Chapter Thirty-Two

He rushed into his boss' office, all out of breath.

"What the hell are you doing here?" Jagger demanded, standing from behind his desk.

Ivan was too out of breath to speak, so he dropped the sack on the table.

"What's this?" Jagger grabbed the bag and looked inside. Then he looked at Ivan. "You better sit, catch your breath, and explain."

Ivan sat and Jagger got him a glass of whiskey.

"Here," he said, "drink this and start talking.

Ivan sat, drank and then started talking very fast.

"Wait, wait, slow down. Adams searched the place?"

"Yes."

"And found the secret compartment?"

"Y-yes."

"How did he know about the office behind the curtain?"

"He-he searched very thoroughly, Boss."

"Ivan," Jagger said, "this is very important. Did he take any of the jewelry?"

"I don't think so," Ivan said.

"Ah, he could've put a piece in his pocket. I'll have to put these in my safe."

He went to the corner of the room, where he had a large, iron box of a safe. He spun the dial, opened it, put the bag in and closed it. Then he stood up, turned and faced Ivan.

"Ivan, I know you're tired, but you've got to go back to town. Saddle a fresh horse from the barn."

"Yes, sir."

"But before that," Jagger went on, "go to the bunkhouse and tell those two men to get Rance and come back here."

"Yes, sir."

"And don't let anyone see you riding back to town," he instructed.

"Right."

Jagger walked Ivan to the front door to be sure he didn't fall down on the way. He opened the front door, but before Ivan left, Martha appeared carrying a canteen.

"Thank you, Martha," Jagger said, handing the canteen to Ivan. He watched as the little man walked to the barn, then closed the door.

From there he went to the kitchen, where Martha was at the stove.

"How's our guest, Martha?"

"He's fine."

"Did he have breakfast?"

"Yes, but he didn't come down for it," Martha said. "I put a tray outside his door. I'm going to do the same with supper when it's ready."

"Very good. Listen, Rance and his boys should be here soon. Let them in."

"Yessir."

Jagger went back to his office and sat behind his desk. He hoped Rance and his men would be back soon. Although he had ostensibly hired Rance as his foreman, there was nothing for him to be foreman of. There were no horses, no cattle, and no ranch hands. There was just Rance and his two gunman buddies. Jagger used them only when he had to, like this afternoon. He couldn't afford to let the doctor look at that dead man too closely. And now he couldn't afford to let Clint Adams find that jewelry, again.

He opened his top drawer and looked at the Colt Paterson sitting inside. It wasn't his style to use a gun, but he realized it might come to that. Hopefully, all the gun work would be taken care of by Rance and his men. But if he needed to use his gun, he would. He had been doing business far too long to let anyone interfere.

He closed the drawer and hoped he could keep it closed.

***

When Clint and Sally came within sight of the house, it was late afternoon. The area around the house quiet.

"It looks quiet," she said.

"That's because it's not a working ranch," Clint said. "There are no ranch hands."

"So, we're just going to ride in?"

"Right up to the front of the house. Come on."

***

They rode up to the house and dismounted. They went up the steps and knocked on the door. It was opened by a thickset, middle-aged woman wearing an apron. Clint figured she was a cook, housekeeper, or both.

"Can I help you?"

"We're here to see Mr. Jagger," Clint said.

"Who shall I say is calling?"

"Clint Adams and Sally Lake."

"And what's it about?"

"Believe me," Clint said. "He knows."

"Wait here, please."

The door closed in their faces."

"Do you really think he's going to let us in?" Sally asked.

"Oh, yes," Clint said. "I think he's just arrogant enough for that."

"I hope you're right."

When the door opened again, she said, "He'll see you. I'll take you to him."

Clint and Sally exchanged looks.

"Sally—"

"Yes, I know.

Chapter Thirty-Three

Martha showed them down a hall to an open door-way, then waved and said, "He is in there," and left without another word.

Clint went through the door before Sally, just in case. Jagger was seated very calmly behind his desk.

"Mr. Adams, Mrs. Lake," he said. "I wish I could say welcome to my home, but this is a bit of an inconvenience. Martha almost has dinner ready, but she did not prepare enough for company."

"We're not here to eat with you, Jagger," Clint said.

"Then what brings you here?"

"We want to have a look around your house," Clint said.

"Is that so?" Jagger asked. "Wouldn't you usually bring a lawman with you for that?"

"Usually," Clint said, "but I think you know Sheriff Barkley wouldn't want to do that."

"So you're hoping I'll just let you search my house?" the undertaker asked.

"I figure if you have nothing to hide, why not?" Clint asked.

Jagger sat back in his chair, folded his hands over his stomach. He was still dressed for a day in town. Maybe he hadn't been home long enough to change. Or maybe he dressed the same every day, home or town.

"You know what?" he said. "I don't see why not. Be my guests. Go ahead and search. Tell Martha I gave you permission I wouldn't want her to try and stop you."

"I wouldn't like that either," Clint said. "She looks pretty formidable."

Jagger laughed and said, "Oh, she is."

***

Clint and Sally started downstairs.

As they walked back to the front, Sally asked, "Are we looking for the jewelry?"

"We're looking for anything incriminating."

They searched the sitting room in front, the dining room, mud room, the entry foyer, which had pieces of furniture in it, and then moved onto the kitchen.

When they entered, Martha was standing at the stove with her back to them.

"Martha, we need to look around in here."

Without turning she said, "As long as you don't ruin my supper."

"We'll be very careful," Clint said.

They looked around, going through drawers of utensils, and cabinets of pots and pans and dry goods.

At one point Martha turned and asked, "Do you want to search the stove? Be careful, it's very hot."

There were pots bubbling on the stove top, and even something in the oven.

"No," Clint said, "that won't be necessary. Looks like you're making a lot of food for one person."

"We have a guest in the house," Martha said.

"Is that a fact?"

Martha compressed her lips. Clint had a feeling she had said something she shouldn't have.

"What room might he be in?" Clint asked. "So we don't bother him when we search upstairs."

Martha considered the question, then said, "First room at the top of the stairs."

"Very good," Clint told her. "We'll avoid that room. Thanks for your help."

He and Sally left the kitchen.

In the dining room Clint said to Sally, "I don't think she was supposed to tell us about their guest."

"Who do you think it is?"

"I don't know, but there's only one way we're going to find out," he said.

"Are we still going to search the upstairs?"

"I think we better," Clint said. "I don't know if we'll even get into this house again.

They walked into the entry foyer to the base of the steps leading upstairs. They went up as quietly as they could. When they reached the top, they saw the only closed door was the first one. They walked past it to the next.

"Looks like there are three other rooms up here," Clint said. "You stay in the hall while I look them over."

"Why? Are you expecting trouble?"

"No, but we don't want whoever's in that room to leave while we're in one of these."

"Oh, gotcha," she said.

They walked to the door of each room, and while Clint went in to search, Sally stood in the hall to watch. Clint went through all the drawers of every chest and dresser. One of the rooms appeared to be Jagger's, as it was the only one with drawers and closets full of clothes.

Clint gave Jagger's room extra special attention, but found nothing in the drawers or closets, or under the bed.

When he came out, he took Sally by the elbow and led her to the closed door.

"Do you think it's locked?" Sally whispered.

"I don't think whoever's inside is a prisoner," Clint said. "Let's just try it."

"You do it," she said.

The door was unlocked. The man inside looked at them in surprise.

"Sally?"

"Omigod!" she blurted. "Charles?"

Chapter Thirty-Four

Charles Lake swung his feet to the floor and got up. He was wearing a very clean white shirt, pressed pants, and was barefoot. His white hair was uncombed, and he had grey stubble on his face. He looked every year of sixty-five Sally said he was.

"What are you doing here, Sally?" he asked.

"I was going to ask you the same thing," Sally said. "I thought you were dead."

"I wanted you to think that."

"But . . .why on earth would you do that? Make me think I woke up next to your corpse."

He sighed and sat down on the bed.

"I wanted to start over," he said.

"You couldn't think of another way?" Clint asked.

"I couldn't—are you the man I've been hearing about? Clint Adams?"

"That's right."

"Well, I wanted to start over, and I didn't want anyone to know I was starting over."

"What's your connection to Jagger?" Clint asked.

"We've been in business together for some time," Lake said. "Not his undertaker business, and not my store, but many other businesses."

"And is that why he helped you?" Clint asked.

"Yes," Lake said, "I wrote a will, in which Sally gets the store and all the money in the banks, but Jagger gets my half of all our business ventures."

"Mr. Lake," Clint said, "you must know the man is a thief. He steals from the dead."

"I don't know any such thing," Lake said. "What he does is his business. I just wanted his help with this."

"Did you know Doctor Saunders?" Sally asked.

"Not well, but I know—what do you mean, *did* I know her?" Lake asked.

"Jagger had her murdered," Sally said. "If he didn't stick a knife in her back, he had one of his men do it."

"I can't believe that," Lake said.

"Tell me something," Clint said. "You faked your death weeks ago. Why are you still here?"

"We needed to work on divesting me of all our business ventures. It'll take a while. But next week I would have been out of here."

"Where are you going?" Sally asked.

"You weren't supposed to know that, Sally," he said. "You were supposed to grieve, and then find someone else. You're still young, my dear. You have a lot of life ahead of you."

"You're damn right I do," she said.

"Then why did you come here?" he asked.

"Jagger stole your things, Charles," she said. "I wanted them back. And I wanted to take your body back to bury in Kansas City."

"What things do you say he stole?"

"Your ring, your watch, your stick pin—"

"But I have those things right here." He leaned over and opened the drawer of the night table. Clint and Sally both looked in and saw his jewelry there. "It was foolish, I know, but these things mean something to me, so I kept them. I didn't think you'd even notice."

"Of course I noticed, Charles, they were your things. They meant something to me, too."

"I-I'm sorry, my dear. I guess I didn't realize."

"And," she said, "I never realized what a selfish man you are!"

***

While Clint and Sally were upstairs, Rance and his men came to the door.

"He's in his office," Martha said, as she let them in.

Rance led the way to Jagger's office.

"Whose horses are outside?" Rance asked.

"Those belong to Clint Adams, and Sally Lake."

"They're here?" Rance asked.

"Yes," Jagger said, "they came to search the house."

"But that means—" Rance started.

"Yes," Jagger said, "they're upstairs right now with Charles Lake."

"That's good," Rance said. "We can take them when they come down."

"No, not here, you fool!" Jagger said. "I don't want any shooting here, but I also don't want them to get back to town. Understand?"

"We understand," Rance said.

"You'll be paid extra, of course."

Jagger never knew the names of the other two men Rance used. They weren't always the same. These two looked much like all the others wearing trail clothes, and low-slung holsters, and greedy looks on their faces.

"You'll have to get your horses out of sight so they don't know you're here when they leave," Jagger said.

"Right." He turned. "Petry, go take the horses around to the back."

"Right."

Petry left the room and ran to the front.

"How do you want this done, Jagger?" Rance asked.

"At this point I just want it done," Jagger said. "I don't care how."

"I know just where we can take 'em," the other man said.

Jagger waved and said, "I don't want to hear about it. I just want to know when it's done."

"Okay, boss," Rance said.

"Now go out the back door in case they come down the stairs," Jagger said. "I'll let you know when they're gone."

"Right," Rance said. "We can catch up and get ahead of them with no problem."

"Then go!"

Chapter Thirty-Five

"What do you want to do now that we've found you?" Clint asked.

"Have I done anything illegal?" Lake asked.

"Well, I don't know if faking your death is considered illegal," Clint said.

"I do," Lake said, "and it's not."

"What about the people who have been killed?" Sally asked.

"I didn't have anything to do with that," Lake said.

"What if Jagger did?" Clint asked.

"Then he can be arrested, not me," Lake said.

"I think I might have to talk to a lawyer," Sally said. "Unless you intend to go ahead with your disappearance."

"All the arrangements have been made," Lake said. "New name, new life—"

"You still intend to go ahead?" Clint asked.

Lake shrugged.

"Why not. As I said, I haven't done anything illegal."

"You're connected to Jagger," Clint pointed out.

"Not anymore," Lake said. "We've dissolved all our partnerships. Now he's just helping me start over, as a friend."

"You think Jagger's doing all this out of friendship?" Clint asked. "I wouldn't be surprised if he's planning on killing you."

"That's ridiculous," Lake said. "Jagger wouldn't do that."

"I don't think you know your partner very well, Mr. Lake."

"And you don't know me very well, either," Sally said. "I'm not going along with this."

Lake frowned.

"That's what I was afraid of, if I had talked to you about this, first."

Sally looked at Clint.

"I don't know what to do now," she said.

"I suppose we should go back to town and see the sheriff. We can let him know what's going on."

Lake looked at the window.

"It's going to be dark, soon," he said. "I'm sure Jagger would put you up for the night."

"Not a chance," Clint said. "I'm not sure we'd ever wake up."

"That's ridiculous," Lake said, standing. "Come on, we'll go talk to him together."

"No," Sally said, "Clint's right, we're heading back to town now to see the sheriff."

Lake sat back down.

"If you insist."

Still looking at Clint she said, "We should take him with us."

"I don't know if we can do that, legally. And I doubt that Jagger would let him go."

"If we leave him here, he'll disappear before we can come back with the law."

"It's not for sure the sheriff would ever come back with us," Clint pointed out. "And you have what you wanted, Sally. To know what happened to your husband, and where his valuables are. You can head home tomorrow, if you want."

"And just let Charles stay dead?" she asked.

"That suits me."

"Sally's right," Clint said. "We'll have to discuss this with a lawyer. And there's still a murder to solve before I leave town. Maybe more than one."

"But you're not a lawman," Lake said. "What do you care?"

"Well," Clint said, "for one thing I knew the doctor. I'm not going to let anyone get away with killing her. And for another, I can't justify leaving and allowing

Jagger to continue stealing from the dead. It's just not right."

"As I said," Lake repeated, "I had nothing to do with that. I just want to get my new life started."

"So do I!" Sally snapped.

"So then you'll go along with the plan?" Lake asked her.

"You know what?" she asked. "Right now, I don't give a damn what you do."

She turned and walked out.

"What about you, Mr. Adams?" Lake asked.

"I haven't made up my mind yet, Mr. Lake," Clint said, "and I don't really think Sally has, either. She's just frustrated."

"Well, I'm sorry, but I've just come too far to change my plans.

"You said you were leaving next week," Clint reminded him. "A lot can happen between now and then."

Clint turned and went out to look for Sally.

***

He found her at the base of the stairs, waiting for him.

"Can we go?"

"I want to see Jagger again," Clint said.

"I'll wait outside," she said.

"I don't want you out there by yourself," he said. "Just wait here. I won't be long."

"Fine!"

She folded her arms and sat on the bottom step.

Clint retraced his steps to Jagger's office and found him there, as they had left him.

"I suppose you discovered our house guest," the undertaker said.

"We did," Clint said. "It was quite a shock to Sally."

"I suppose knowing your husband would rather be dead than with you is a shock."

"Jagger, did you investigate the legality of this? Faking a man's death?"

"I did not," Jagger said. "I left that to Charles. He's satisfied he's not breaking any laws."

"Well, I'm not that sure," Clint said, "so I'll be talking to the sheriff and a lawyer when we get back to Hays."

"That's up to you, sir."

Clint decided to go on keeping quiet about the death of the doctor. Maybe Jagger would give himself away, eventually.

"Would you like to stay the night and head back in the morning?" Jagger asked.

"No thanks. It's not that long of a ride." Besides, I don't know what would happen during the night."

"I'm sorry you feel that way, Adams. I hope you'll be leaving town as soon as possible."

"As soon as I get all this settled," Clint said. "If I can put you away, Jagger, I will."

Jagger smiled.

"You're welcome to try."

***

Clint rejoined Sally at the steps, helped her up to her feet.

"Are you all right?"

"No, I'm not," she said. "I just found out my husband would rather be dead then spend one more minute with me. How do you think that makes me feel?"

"I can't imagine."

He didn't tell her that Jagger had mentioned the same thing.

"But just for the record," he said, "I think he's a complete fool."

"Thank you."

"Let's get on our horses and see if we can get back to town without either of them stepping in a chuckhole in the dark," Clint said.

As they went out the door to their mounts, Sally said, "Well, thank you for giving me a whole new problem to worry about."

Chapter Thirty-Six

After Clint and Sally left the house, Jagger went to the back door. He found Rance and his men there, smoking.

"They just left," he told Rance. "You and your boys get moving."

"Yes, sir."

"And don't come back here until it's done."

"Right." Rance turned to his men. "Mount up."

Jagger watched as the men rode away. He hoped he was one night from this all being over so he could get back to work.

Oh, and there was a guest to take care of.

***

Clint and Sally rode in the dark at as decent a pace as they could, helped by a three-quarter moon. The Tobiano was surefooted, but Clint didn't know about Sally's mount. It wasn't the same one they brought with them from Kansas City.

"My horse doesn't feel steady," Sally said.

"Just follow me closely," Clint said. "Mine's steady."

"I'm glad one of us is," she said.

***

Rance and his men made good time, because they all knew the way, even in the dark.

"Come on, Petry," Rance said. "Where's the ambush spot?"

"Just up ahead," Petry said. "If they stay on the road, they've got to go through this pass. Two of us on one side and one on the other."

"You take the other," Rance said. "I'll take Dave with me."

"Right."

***

Clint drew his horse to a stop.

"What's wrong?" Sally asked.

"I don't know," Clint said. "I just don't feel right."

"About what?"

"About Jagger letting us get back to town, when he knows we'll talk to the sheriff."

"Somebody following us?" she asked.

"No," Clint said, "I'd feel that. Or hear them."

"Then what is it?"

"If I'm not mistaken, there's a short pass up ahead, just long enough for a good ambush."

"Can we get to town without going through that pass?" she asked.

"If I knew the area better, I could answer that," Clint said. "As it is, I don't want to try it in the dark."

"So what do we do?"

"You dismount and take your horse into those trees," Clint said. "Don't move out until I come back."

"What are you going to do?"

"I'm going to ride up ahead and check out that pass," he explained.

"And if I hear shots?"

"Stay where you are."

"And if you don't come back?" she asked.

"I'll come back."

"Clint," she said, "I've already had one man disappoint me today. If you don't come back, I'm out here all alone."

"All right, then," Clint said. "Come with me but do exactly as I say."

"Of course."

"And be ready to use that gun I gave you," he added, "even if I just need you to make some noise."

"Make some noise." She nodded. "I can do that."

Chapter Thirty-Seven

Clint moved forward at a much slower pace.

"Clint—" Sally started.

"Shhh." He kept his voice down. "Don't talk. I need to listen."

She snapped her lips shut.

***

Up ahead Rance and Dave were on one side of the short pass, with Petry on the other. Rance thought he had made a good choice. Once Adams and the girl were in the pass, they were done.

"How long—" Dave started, but Rance turned and slapped him to keep him quiet.

Dave was getting a cramp in his leg. He stretched it out to try and ease it, but his boot heel dislodged a large rock. It went rolling down the side to the ground.

"Jesus!" Rance hissed.

"Sorry," Dave said continuing to flex his leg.

"Hold still and keep quiet!" Rance snapped.

But it was too late . . .

***

Clint heard the rock roll down and hit the ground. He held up his hand to stop Sally's progress as he reined his Tobiano in.

"Did you hear that?" he whispered.

"Hear what?"

"I heard a rock roll and hit the ground."

"From the pass?" she asked.

"It's got to be."

"What do we do?"

"We've got to remember, if it's dark for us, it's dark for them too."

"So?"

"The only way to see them is a muzzle flash. Same for them, they need a muzzle flash to shoot at. We're not going to give them one. Not an accurate one, anyway."

"How do you mean?"

"When we get to the mouth of the pass, you dismount, pull your horse to the side where he won't be seen. Then get down nice and low, take out your gun. When I signal, I want you to hold it up and pull the trigger."

"You want me to give them a muzzle flash to shoot at."

"Right," he said. "Then when I see their flashes, I'll do the rest."

"Wait a minute," she said. "Who are they going to think I'm shooting at?"

"Don't worry," he said. "One of them will think you're shooting at him, and he'll shoot back. That'll spook the others into shooting, too. Then I've got them."

"You're that sure of yourself?" she asked. "That you can hit them in the dark?"

"I've done this before, Sally. Just trust me. You fire once, then take cover. Don't come out until I tell you."

"And what's your signal that I should shoot?"

"I'll whistle."

"They won't hear it?"

"It won't matter," he said. "Once I whistle and you fire, all hell is going to shake loose."

"What if we're wrong?" she asked. "What if nobody's waiting in the pass?"

"Then we'll just ride through," Clint said. "But I don't think Jagger wants us back in town. Are you ready?

"Sure."

"Dismount and pull your horse over to one side. Then come back here and get on your knees."

"This is not where I expected you to ever tell me that."

"You're a dirty girl," he said, with a smirk.

When Sally was in position Clint started his horse forward. He knew they'd hear the horses' hooves on the rock floor of the pass, but they still wouldn't see him because of the shadow in the pass.

When Clint got far enough into the pass, he whistled; Sally's shot followed closely, creating a clear muzzle flash.

***

Dave was still flexing his cramping leg. He wished this was over so he could stand up.

"Sit still!" Rance hissed at him.

"My leg hurts!"

"You damned—" Rance started, but then he heard a whistle, and then a shot.

"Don't—" he started to warn Dave, not wanting the man to shoot, but it was too late.

"There he is!" Dave shouted. He stood and fired at the muzzle flash, creating one of his own.

"Damn it!" Rance swore when he heard Petry fire, as well.

Rance holstered his gun and ran for his horse. This ambush was busted.

***

Clint saw the first muzzle flash and fired. He heard a grunt as his lead hit flesh. Then he heard a body rolling down to the pass floor. Then came the second flash, as somebody on the other side fired at his. He had to hope the shot wasn't accurate, and he was almost unlucky. He heard the lead whiz past his ear, and then he fired at the second flash. He didn't hear anything to indicate his shot was accurate, until another body rolled down to the floor.

He didn't know how many more there might be, but hitting two of them in the dark was going to spook them.

He wheeled his horse around and rode back to the mouth of the pass.

"Sally, come on!"

She hurried to her horse and mounted it.

"Let's ride!" he called to her.

They started through the pass at breakneck speed. Clint was waiting for more shots, but they didn't come. In moments they were out of the pass, back on the road to town.

He kept riding, hoping Sally wouldn't slow down until they reached the city limits.

Chapter Thirty-Eight

Clint and Sally rode to the livery and unsaddled their horses themselves, as the hostler was fast asleep.

"Do you think the sheriff is in his office?" Sally asked.

"Believe me," Clint said, since the sheriff lived there, "he's in his office."

When they got there, Clint pounded on the door. The sheriff answered it, holding a coffee mug.

"You're back," he said. "Come on in."

Clint and Sally stepped in, and the lawman locked the door.

"We could use some of that coffee," Clint told him.

"This ain't actually coffee," Barkley said. "I was havin' a drink."

"I could use a drink," Sally said.

"I'll pass," Clint said.

"Good, 'cause I only got one more mug."

He went to his desk, took out the second mug and the bottle and poured Sally a drink.

"Thank you," she said. "I need this."

"Somethin' go wrong?" he asked, while she sipped.

"My husband is still alive and some of Jagger's men tried to kill us."

"Sounds like you need to sit down," Barkley said. "Be my guest." He pointed to his chair, behind the desk.

"Thank you, Sheriff."

He looked at Clint,

"I guess you better tell me what happened."

He perched his hip on his desk and Clint told him everything in order.

"Jesus," he said when Clint was done. "To tell you the truth, I don't actually know if it's illegal to fake your own death."

"I'm sure there's a lawyer in town who can answer legal questions," Clint said.

"There are a few," Barkley said. "And more every day. You'll just need to use one who doesn't work for Jagger."

"Good," Clint said, "then there'll be one who doesn't work for Jagger."

"That's for sure," the lawman said. "At first light I'll go out with some men and retrieve those you shot. Maybe I'll know who they work for."

"I think we'll know who they work for," Sally said.

"Still," Barkley said, "I'd need evidence that Jagger sent them after you."

"Maybe one of them is still alive," Sally offered.

"That'd be helpful." Clint said to the sheriff. "I'll go with you."

"Did you tell Jagger about Doc Saunders bein' killed?"

"No, we didn't mention it. I'm still waiting for him to give himself away."

"So then, your husband didn't know she was dead?"

"If he knew it, he didn't mention it."

"Well," the sheriff said, "at least you got all the answers you came here lookin' for, Mrs. Lake."

"Maybe," Sally said, "but now I've got some new ones, and I'm not leaving town without answers."

"And the same goes for you, huh?"

"That's right."

"Well, we're closer," Barkley said, "but I still need evidence. "I'll pick you up in front of your hotel at eight a.m. and we'll ride out for those bodies."

"I'll be there," Clint said.

He and Sally left the sheriff's office and went to their hotel.

***

"I'd invite you in, but . . ." Sally said, when they got to their doors.

191

"I understand," he said. "It's been a tough day. I'll come and see you after the sheriff and I get back from collecting those bodies."

"I'll be waiting for you."

Chapter Thirty-Nine

Clint came out of the hotel early enough to collect his Tobiano from the livery. He walked the horse back to the hotel, found the sheriff and a deputy there, with another man driving a buckboard.

"Ready?" Barkley asked.

"I'm ready."

He mounted up and they rode out.

***

Jagger was angry.

Rance had returned the night before, told him they had not killed the Gunsmith, and his two men were dead.

"You're sure they're dead?" the undertaker asked.

"Yes, sir," Rance lied.

He wasn't sure at all. It had been too dark. He knew they were shot, but couldn't be sure they were dead.

Jagger told Rance to go to the bunkhouse and he would see him in the morning.

***

In the morning Jagger told Martha to call Charles Lake down for breakfast.

When Lake appeared he said, "Sit down, Charles."

Lake, still dressed as he had been when Clint and Sally saw him, sat.

"How did it go between you and your wife last night?" Jagger asked.

"Not well," Lake said. "She doesn't understand."

"I didn't think she would," Jagger said, "but you insisted."

"Let's not go through this again, Jagger," Lake said.

"No, no, you're quite right," Jagger said. "Everything is in place for your rebirth, so let's have breakfast, dot the 'I's' and cross the 't's'."

Martha appeared and set a plate of flapjacks in front of Lake.

"I'm really not that hungry—" Lake started.

Jagger waved him silent until Martha went back to the kitchen.

"You don't want to insult her," Jagger said, when she was gone. "So put some syrup on those cakes and eat them while we talk."

"Yes, all right," Lake said. He reached for the syrup mug, doused the flapjacks and started eating . . .

***

When Martha came back into the dining room, Lake's head was on the table, almost in the plate of flapjacks.

"You can remove the dishes, Martha," Jagger said. "He's quite dead."

"Yes, sir."

While Martha cleared the table, Jagger considered his options for disposing of Charles Lake's body. Actually, killing him had been moved up since Adams and Sally Lake had found him there. But killing him was no problem, because to the outside world, he was already dead. True, Adams and the woman had found him, but no one else had seen him, and they would never be able to prove he was alive. Even if Clint Adams and Sally Lake came back with the sheriff, Lake would be gone by then.

Of course, all would have been well if Rance and his men had accomplished their task. Now he was going to have to come up with another plan to get rid of them. Even though they could not prove anything against him, he didn't want them to keep trying. He had to put a stop to all this.

The easy way would have been to have them spend the night, and then have one of Martha's special plates of flapjacks. Too bad he wasn't able to convince them to accept his invitation the night before. At this point in the proceedings, Jagger wasn't sure whose side Sheriff Barkley was on, and if Adams and the woman could convince him to ride out to the house.

Then Jagger realized he had made a mistake. He needed to send Rance out to recover the bodies of his two men, before Adams got the sheriff to go out and do that.

He left the dining room table and rushed out to the bunk house.

***

Rance was lying on a bunk, extremely unhappy about how things had gone at the pass. He had underestimated Clint Adams, feeling that the dark would make him an easy target. But even at his age, he had lived up to his Gunsmith reputation. Rance knew he was going to need more men to get the job done. Unfortunately, he didn't have any at the moment. He would have to go to a nearby town to recruit some—if Jagger gave him the time to redeem himself.

At that very moment the bunkhouse door opened, and Jagger entered. Since this had never happened before, Rance leaped to his feet.

"Rance!" Jagger shouted. "You've gotta get out there and either bring back the bodies or bury 'em. I don't want Clint Adams recovering them."

"Now?"

"Right now!"

"I don't have any men to take with me," Rance said.

"And who's fault is that?" Jagger demanded and left, slamming the door behind him.

Chapter Forty

As Clint, the sheriff and his men left Hays at eight a.m., Rance reached the pass, dismounted and went to find the bodies of his two men. The man who had been with him had obviously died right away, but Petry—who had chosen this spot for the ambush—showed signs of having been alive when he hit the floor of the pass. There was enough loose ground to show that he had crawled some after landing, but he was dead now.

"Sorry, Petry," Rance said, realizing he might have been able to save the man if he had found him there alive and moved him. But he was concerned with saving his own life now.

He dragged both bodies from the pass, found softer ground and started using the shovel he had brought with him.

***

"Hang on!" Clint called out, holding up a hand.

Sheriff Barkley and his deputy stopped, and the man driving the buckboard reined in his horse.

"What is it?" Barkley asked.

"I hear something."

"Over the noise this buckboard is makin'?" the deputy asked.

"The buckboard is behind us," Clint said to the young man. "I hear noise up ahead."

"What kind of noise?" Barkley asked.

"Just listen."

They all listened intently. The man driving the buckboard was too far back. The young deputy strained but heard nothing.

"You hear it?" Clint asked the sheriff.

"Yes," Barkley said, brightening. "It sounds like a shovel."

"Someone's diggin' a hole?" the deputy asked.

"A hole or two," Clint said.

"Somebody's diggin' graves," Barkley said.

"Jagger doesn't want anyone else recovering those dead men," Clint said. He turned in his saddle. "You two stay here." Then he looked at Sheriff Barkley. "Let's ride slowly. Hopefully, he's making enough noise, he won't hear us."

They started into the pass. When they got halfway Clint said, "Let's dismount."

They did so, grounded the reins and continued on foot. As they got closer to the other end of the pass, the digging noises got louder.

When they came out the mouth of the pass, the sound was much clearer, and they were able to locate it.

"That way," Clint said, pointing.

They moved slowly toward the sound, Clint ready to draw his gun, and Berkley with his gun in hand.

Eventually they came up behind Rance while he was still digging. His two partner's bodies were piled alongside him. He was apparently digging one grave for the two of them.

"Hold it right there," Barkley said.

Rance froze, then looked over his shoulder.

"Rance," Barkley said recognizing him.

"You know him?" Clint asked.

"I do," the lawman said. "He works for Jagger."

"Then that's what we need," Clint said. "You can bring Jagger in."

"That depends on what Rance has to say."

Still holding the shovel, Rance said, "I ain't sayin' nothin'."

"I think you are," Clint said.

"Why would I?" Rance asked.

"Because that hole is big enough for three bodies. Don't you agree, Sheriff."

"Looks big enough to me," Barkley said.

"Rance," Clint said, "I think you should put that shovel down before you try to do something stupid with it."

Rance looked like he was caught in the act.

"Drop it," Clint said.

He dropped it."

"Now get out of that hole," Barkley said. "We won't need it. We're takin' all three of you back to town."

"I ain't gonna say nothin'," Rance said.

"We can always bring you back out here," Clint said. "You'll be awful lonely in that hole."

Rance looked at Barkley.

"You ain't gonna let him kill me," he said.

"He's the Gunsmith, Rance," the sheriff said. "How would you suggest I stop him?"

"Come on," Clint said, "let's get that buckboard up here. Rance can load the bodies on it."

"Jagger will kill me if he finds out," Rance complained.

"I can kill you right now, if you prefer. Take your pick."

Rance grimaced and said, "I'll wait."

Clint looked at Barkley.

"I'll wait here with him. You get the others to bring the buckboard up."

"Right."

The lawman rode back into the pass and out the other side, returned with the deputy and the buckboard.

"Get those bodies loaded up," Clint told Rance.

"I'll help 'im," the deputy said.

"Suit yourself," Clint said.

Rance and the deputy—whose name Clint still didn't know—carried the bodies to the buckboard and loaded them on.

"Now tie him up and put him back there with his friend," Clint said.

"I gotta ride with the dead?" Rance asked.

"Hey," Clint said, "they were your friends, right?"

Chapter Forty-One

When they got back to town they drove the buckboard over to the undertaker's, to drop the bodies off with Ivan.

"You recognize them?" Clint asked.

"No, sir," Ivan said, as they put the bodies in the back room.

"Do you recognize him?" Clint asked, pointing at Rance.

"Uh, yes, sir."

"I thought you might. Come on, we're going over to the sheriff's office."

The sheriff was waiting for them, having dropped his horse at the livery.

"Come on in," Barkley said to Rance. "I've got a nice cell waitin' for you."

"What's the charge?" Rance demanded, as Barkley locked the door.

"Attempted murder," the lawman said, "and maybe murder later."

"Who'd I murder?"

"Let's try Doc Saunders, for one," Barkley said.

He locked the door and left the cell block.

Clint gestured with a coffee cup and said, "helped myself. Hope you don't mind."

"Not at all." Barkley got himself a cup and sat at his desk. "Whataya wanna do now?"

"Talk to a lawyer," Clint said, "after breakfast. Then, if you're willing, I'd like you to ride out to Jagger's ranch with me."

"I guess it's about time I do my job," Barkley said. "I'll be ready when you are."

"Then I'll see you in a while. I'll want to talk to Rance a bit before we go," Clint said and left.

***

When Sally saw Clint standing in the hall, she threw her arms around him.

"I'm so glad to see you," she said, hugging him tightly.

"Let's get out of the hall," he said, and walked her into the room, closing the door behind them. "You must be pretty hungry."

She held him tight for a few more seconds, then released him and stepped back.

"Right," she said, "that's what I mean. I'm glad to see you, and now we can eat."

"Well, let's go, then," Clint said. "I'm kind of hungry, myself."

***

Over breakfast in the hotel, Clint filled Sally in on what happened out at the pass.

"So you did kill two of them," Sally said.

"Looks like it. And the third one came back to bury them."

"Why would he do that?" she asked.

"I think it's likely Jagger sent him back to hide them before we could get there."

"Only he didn't make it in time."

"Almost," Clint said. "He had a nice hole dug, big enough for the two of them. And there would have been no marker."

"Good, they didn't deserve any."

"Well, we didn't leave them buried out there," Clint told her.

"Did he know them?"

"He says he didn't, but I think it's likely he did."

"Do you think Jagger will be coming to town this morning?" she asked.

"Probably not until he's heard from Rance."

"But he won't."

"Rance is in jail," Clint said. "Jagger's going to hear from the sheriff and me."

"Is the sheriff going to arrest him?"

"Not until I talk with a lawyer."

"When will you do that?"

"I'll find one right after breakfast."

"Well, I'm not staying in my room again," she said. "I'll come with you."

"You might as well," Clint said. "We'll be talking about your husband."

***

After breakfast Clint and Sally left the hotel in search of a lawyer. Clint didn't care which one he used, he just needed some legal questions answered, so he figured to stop into the first office they came to.

"You think we're just going to find a lawyer's office this way?" Sally asked.

"If Hays wants to grow, they're going to need everything, including lawyers. We'll find one."

After about an hour of walking, Clint pointed and said, "There's a shingle."

"William Armitage, Attorney-at-Law," Sally said.

"That's our man."

They walked up to the front door and found it unlocked. When they stepped inside, they saw a small office with a young man seated at a desk.

"Good morning," the man said. "What can I do for you folks."

"As long as you're the lawyer, Mr. Armitage, I have some questions to ask."

"I'm a lawyer," the man said, "and I'm Armitage, so I'll see if I can answer them for you."

"My first question is: do you have a client named Charles Jagger?"

"The undertaker?" Armitage made a face. "I don't work for him, and never would. He's as crooked as they come."

"That's what we've found out," Clint said, "only we can't prove anything."

"So you've dealt with him already?"

"We have."

"Then have a seat and tell me what I can do for you folks," the lawyer invited.

Clint and Sally sat down and told the lawyer the whole story...

Chapter Forty-Two

"If your husband faked his own death, Mrs. Lake," Armitage said, "then he was committing fraud, and that's against the law."

"I knew it!" she said.

"Does this have something to do with Jagger?" Armitage asked.

"It does," Clint said. "He helped Lake fake his death."

"Then he broke the law, too."

"That's what I wanted to know," Clint said.

"Are you going to get the sheriff to arrest him?"

"He said he would if I could prove it," Clint said. "And we've got one of his men in a cell."

"Well, if you're going to need a lawyer, I'm your man."

"If you've got the time," Clint said.

"I just opened my office two weeks ago. I don't even have a secretary, yet. I've got time."

"Okay," Clint said, "I'll keep you in mind."

"What're you going to do now?" Armitage asked.

"We're going to finish this thing up with Jagger and then I'll take Sally back to Kansas City."

"Mrs. Lake," Armitage said, "if you change your mind about leaving Hays, I could sure use a secretary."

Sally smiled at him and said, "I'll keep that in mind, too."

They left the lawyer's office and headed for the sheriff.

***

Barkley listened to what they had learned from the lawyer.

"So, I figure you've got enough to ride out there and take Jagger into custody." Clint finished.

Barkley stroked his jaw.

"Yeah, it sounds like it, I guess. But maybe we should check and see if Judge Crenshaw is afraid of Jagger or not."

"Why don't you do that, Sheriff?" Clint asked. "We'll meet you in front of our hotel."

"Okay," Barkley said, "let me get my deputy to sit here and watch Rance."

"Right."

They all left the office at the same time.

***

"I haven't heard anything about this Judge Crenshaw since we've been in town," Sally said, as they walked to the hotel, leading their horses.

"We could ask Mr. Armitage about him, but I'd like to get moving."

"The handsome young lawyer?" she said. "I could ask him and meet you at the hotel."

"Okay, you do that," Clint said, "just don't take too long."

"That'll depend," she said.

"On what?"

She smiled and said, "On whether he's married or not."

***

Clint walked to the hotel, tied the Tobiano off and then sat on the porch to wait.

Sally came back within the hour, looking flushed.

"How'd it go?" Clint asked.

"He is very willing to help," she said. "Where's the sheriff?"

"He's checking in with the judge. He'll meet us here."

Sally sat next to Clint on the porch.

***

While Clint and Sally waited for the sheriff, Ivan once again saddled his horse and rode out to tell Jagger about his men. He thought his boss would be interested to know that two of them were dead, and one was in jail, probably talking.

***

When Ivan arrived at Jagger's house, the undertaker, seated at his desk, listened to what he had to say. When Ivan was done, Jagger opened a top drawer and took out a sheaf of papers. He leafed through them quickly, then stopped at the last page and said to Ivan, "Come here."

Ivan crossed the room and stood next to the desk.

"Sign here," Jagger told him.

Ivan took the pen and signed his name.

Jagger turned the papers around and also signed his name, then handed the papers to Ivan.

"It's yours," he said.

"Sir?"

"The undertaking business," Jagger said, "you own it. I won't be around much longer. Now get on back to town."

Yes, Boss," he said, and started for the door.

"Ivan!"

The little man turned.

"You're your own boss, now."

"Yes, sir."

"Send Martha in on your way out."

While he waited for Martha, he took some more papers from his desk and started signing them. When Martha came in he said, "Sit down."

She sat across his desk from him. He came around and set a stack of papers down.

"Sign these."

"What are they?"

"Your reward for years of service," he said.

After she finished signing all the papers he had put in front of her he said, "Now it's time for breakfast . . ."

***

When the sheriff came to the hotel he told Clint, "The judge is in on this, with us."

"Then let's go," Clint said.

The three men mounted up and rode out of town.

When they reached Charles Jagger's house, they dismounted and knocked on the front door. It was opened by Martha.

"We're here to see Mr. Jagger, Martha," Clint said.

"He's having breakfast." she turned and walked away, leaving the door open.

"I guess that's an invitation," Barkley said.

Since he was the man with the badge, Clint allowed him to walk in first, then followed with Sally.

When they reached the dining room, Martha was standing next to Jagger's chair. Her boss was sitting with his head on the table.

"What's goin' on?" the sheriff asked.

"He knew you were coming, so he wanted breakfast," she said.

Barkley leaned over Jagger, then looked at Clint and said, "He's dead."

"And there's not a mark on him," Clint said. Then he looked at Martha. "What did he have for breakfast?"

"He told me to make my special pancakes."

Now Available!

THE GUNSMITH
BOOKS 430 – 484

For more information
visit: www.SpeakingVolumes.us

Now Available!

ROBERT J. RANDISI'S
RAT PACK MYSTERIES

GET SWEPT AWAY INTO
THE LAS VEGAS ERA OF THE 60s

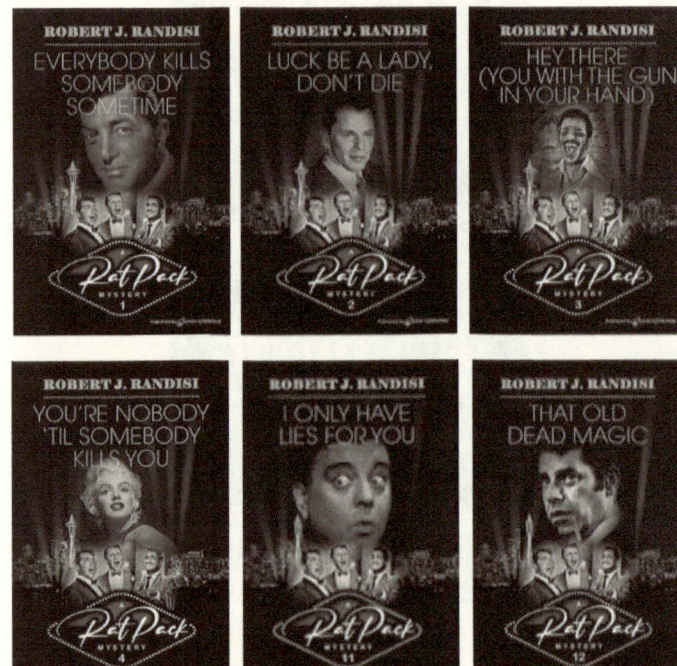

For more information
visit: www.SpeakingVolumes.us

Now Available!

THE GUNSMITH GIANT SERIES

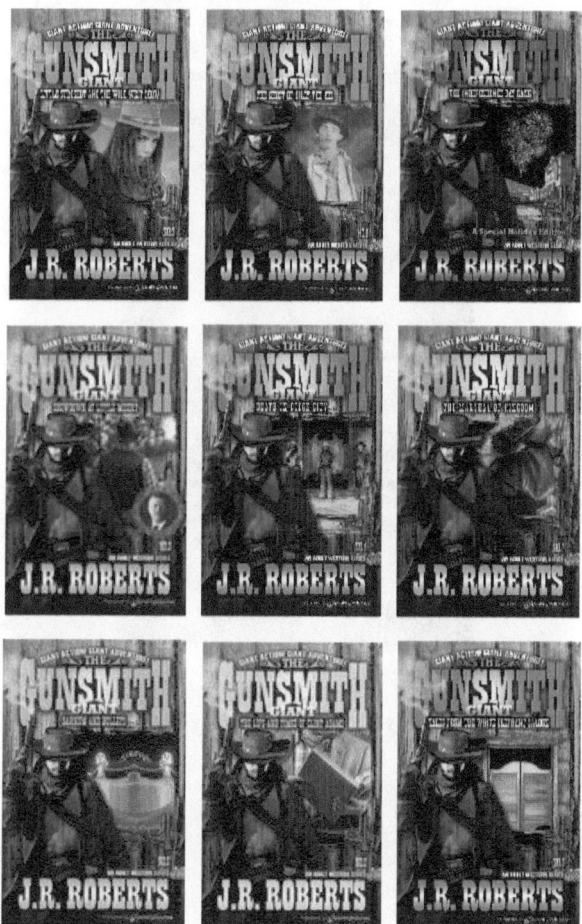

For more information
visit: www.SpeakingVolumes.us

Now Available!

AWARD-WINNING AUTHOR
ROBERT J. RANDISI (J.R. ROBERTS)

For more information
visit: www.SpeakingVolumes.us